WAKE

Connor Lindstrom

ISBN-13: 978-0-6451-6730-6

So are we each lit briefly by engulfments

Of space like the worm in the beak of

the bird, yielding to sudden corridors

of light-into-light, never asking: *why*

tell me why

   all this light?

\-   Tess Gallagher, *My Unopened Life*

Contents

Alight

I

The sound of the doorbell echoed through the house, followed by the shuffling of heavy feet and rattling of keys.

The door was swung open by a very large man with wiry chest hairs popping over the neck of his polo shirt. He sported a blonde mullet and wore a toothy smile.

"Well now, you must be Joey, aye?" asked the large man.

"Yes," Joey replied, "And you must be Robert?"

"Ahhhweee, did my missus list my name as Robert? Just call me Bob! Nobody calls me Robert, except for maybe my old man, but he's six foot under now!"

Bob rocked back on his heels and laughed so hard that Joey thought she heard the furniture in the corridor topple over.

"Oooohweee!" exclaimed Bob, wiping happy tears from his bloodshot eyes. "Well come on, why don't you meet Mazzy."

Bob ducked under the front doorway and led Joey over a weed-infested lawn to the garage. He pulled a key chain from his pocket, picked a purple key from the bunch and jangled it into the lock. The garage door rolled open to reveal a navy 1981 Volvo station wagon.

"Mazzy!" Bob declared. "Ain't she just beau-ti-ful!"

Joey didn't think Mazzy was particularly beautiful. The car was old and rusted and covered in dust. But as soon as Joey saw the car advertised online, she knew she had to have it. After all, she had been searching for this model since she received her license two years ago. Joey's mum had owned a navy 1981 Volvo station wagon before it was crumpled under an oncoming B-double, driven by a man named Pete, who had dozed off at the wheel. Pete survived the crash. Joey's mum, and dad, did not.

"Do you mind if I rename the car?" Joey asked politely.

A plume of vapour rose from Bob's mouth. *Pineapple Ice*. Joey knew the flavour well. Her roommate from boarding school, Christina, would smoke it after lights out. It was her pacifier. The vapour would float up from Christina's bottom bunk and drift into Joey's nostrils. *The quintessential scent of the tropics*. Joey would lie awake imagining that she was dancing on a secluded beach surrounded by turquoise water and lush palm trees, far away from the drab tedium of Chelton Grammar School for Girls.

"What? Doesn't look like a Mazzy to you?" Bob chuckled.

"No," Joey said, "I want to call it Sylvia."

"Well, as soon as you give me the cash, darl, you can call it whatever the fuck ya want!"

Joey swung her backpack off her shoulder and pulled out two rolls of fifty-dollar notes, twenty notes a roll, strapped with red rubber bands. Joey had just turned eighteen, a week after graduating high school. In their will, Joey's parents had permitted their daughter access to her inherence once she turned eighteen. Before that age, Joey's money was controlled by her Aunt Susie, the younger sister of Joey's mother, Sylvia. It was Aunt Susie's idea to send Joey to an elite all-girls boarding school in the Victorian countryside. Aunt Susie thought it would help Joey grow into a fine young woman. Joey knew Aunt Susie only sent her there to evade any domestic obligations involved in the care of her niece.

Joey handed Bob the two thousand dollars. This was the price that his wife had advertised the car for online.

"You must be a hard saver!" Bob gawked.

Joey just nodded. "Keys?"

"Straight to business! I like it!"

Bob shot her a cheeky grin and reached into his back pocket to retrieve the car keys. But then he hesitated.

"I wanna be honest with ya, Joey, because you seem like a real nice girl. I don't know what me missus wrote in that ad, but the left tail light ain't workin'. There's also a suspect brown stain on the back seat – don't ask. But apart from that, she runs like the clappers and she's got enough space in the boot for an orgy."

Joey stiffened.

"Ahh, I'm only yanking ya chain love!" Bob boomed, before keeling over in a fit of laughter.

Unamused, Joey swung her backpack over her shoulder and climbed into the driver's seat, pulling the door behind her with a heavy thunk. The engine grumbled to a start. With her window wound down, Joey reversed the car in the gravel driveway and slowed as Bob approached.

"Drive safe darlin'," Bob said.

"Thanks Bob," Joey said, before adding, "Oh Bob, just one more thing?"

"Yeah?"

"Can I throw in an extra ten for the vape?"

Bob placed the vape in Joey's hand.

"You can have it for free. It's me missus that's got me on these fruity fuckin' vapes. I'd much prefer a dart, but she's convinced these are better for my health. It seems I don't know a fuckin' thing anymore!"

"Yeah... well, thanks Bob," was all Joey could manage.

She took a long draw from the vape, sucking the Pineapple Ice deep into the lower chambers of her lungs before pulling out of Bob's driveway and onto the main road. The nicotine head spin came with a fleeting vision of the tropics that eventually dissolved into the wide-open road. Sylvia coughed and spluttered, clouds of smoke kicking up behind her rusted rear bumper. The unceasing bitumen presented possibility for Joey. Possibility that she had only ever dreamed of. Home on the road. *My home*, Joey thought, as she switched the air conditioning on high, expelling a small storm of dust. She sneezed and nearly veered off the road before correcting herself and gunning it towards the horizon.

II

Deborah read in *The Age* that January had been the hottest month on record, with temperatures expected to climb further over the coming weeks. Not even the wind could offer reprieve from the heat of the day. When the wind did come, it was like being stuck inside a giant hairdryer.

Andrew, Deborah's husband, refused to pay for air conditioning. He told "Deb," as he called her (a name that she vehemently protested against – she thought it made her sound like a deli spread), that if she was really that hot, then she could take her clothes off. Raised in a modest Catholic home, Deborah always felt uncomfortable in the nude. But tonight, she would rail against the Catholic sensibilities of propriety and purity that were inculcated in her as a child by the local bishop.

Three years ago, when Deborah and Andrew were having sex on a semi-regular basis, Deborah would refuse to turn on the lights. She felt sexier in the dark. Tonight, she would strip down to just her bra and panties. Deborah hoped that for their five-year wedding anniversary, her Big Reveal would rekindle – no, reignite – the Spark that had been blown out of their relationship.

Andrew claimed that he did not want to do anything *special*. He told Deborah that just a couple of beers and a steak would suffice, that she didn't have to *try* so hard to make him happy. Deborah thought back to what her mother told her and her three sisters from a young age – *the magic in a relationship dies when the woman stops trying*. Deborah found it difficult to *try* for a man who did not *try* for her.

In front of the large mirror in her bedroom, Deborah winged the tips of her eyeliner and propped up her breasts in her best bra. She wasn't sure if this was her mother's idea of *trying*, but she figured that this would appeal to Andrew's carnal desires. Andrew was a simple man after all. When the pair were first married five years ago, he could achieve an erection when Deborah said words like "soft" and "wet" and "tight," even when spoken outside of a sexual context. He also got hard when Deborah bent over to fill the bowls of their two sheepdogs, Bert and Ernie, with kibble. Deborah always knew it was there; she could hear the rush of blood.

Now, Andrew's enthusiasm for Deborah had all but vanished. He looked at her like a friend he shared a bed with, not a woman capable of stirring fervour in the loins. Deborah painted her lips red and smacked them together. She stared at her made-up face in the mirror, then began to cry. The sun that streamed through her bedroom window cast a yellow light across the caesarean scar that snaked its way above her black panties. From the front porch, she could hear the dogs barking at the sound of Andrew's ute grunting up the long dirt driveway. Deborah pulled her underwear up to cover the scar and wiped her tears. There was no time for theatrics if this was to be her last *try*. Besides, perhaps it was just the heat that was bringing Deborah to tears; the heat that had begun to close in all around.

III

It was a humble campsite, situated about an hour or so north of Melbourne. Joey searched "campsite" on her phone, and this is where the lady with the monotone voice directed her. The campsite consisted of a block of unisex toilets and a couple of permanently fixed barbecues with grills caked in lunchtime meat residue. What the campsite lacked in facilities, it made up for in natural beauty. It lay at the foot of a valley, flanked by mountains covered in bright green foliage. A steady stream of water trickled its way down the ridge of one of the mountains, slushing over mossy rocks and broken sticks before pooling into a creek near the campsite where children swum and nervous mothers watched on, hawk-eyed.

Joey sat in the boot of Sylvia. The place was crawling with revellers – from young families hastily erecting tents before nightfall to grey nomads parked up in campervans, sipping on chilled beers straight from their bar fridges. Joey directed her gaze to a family sitting amicably around a squat plastic table, the parents sharing a bottle of wine, the kids sipping on cans of Kirks Lemonade. The mother rose from her camping chair and sprayed mosquito repellent on the legs of her children without them even looking up from their electronic devices. Joey overhead the mother assert that screen time would rot her children's precious brains. They handed their devices over as if they were soldiers surrendering their weapons to the enemy. Joey, still navigating her nascent adult world of moral relativism and existential meaning, longed for this kind of direction and wisdom from elders, which she so sorely missed as a child.

This was with exception to Aunt Susie, who would impart her unsolicited "wisdom" when she called Joey once a month due to boredom or loneliness. Wisdom like: all men are selfish pigs, immigrants steal Australian jobs, and a bad vaccine was what caused cousin Danny to develop autism. If either one of Joey's parents had passed on any Wisdom to her, she couldn't remember it. She was seven when they died. All she remembered was that her mother wore flowers in her hair and that her father had a soft voice.

During school holidays, her roommate Christina would invite Joey to stay with her family at their beachfront property in Lorne. Joey would wake up to the smell of the ocean and eggs frying on the pan. She'd fly kites on the beach with Christina's little sister, Kaylan. At night, Joey would play charades with the family. Joey would always win. Christina's mum was so impressed with Joey's ability to pantomime titles of books, movies and songs that she suggested Joey would make a terrific actor. This was the first time anyone, as far back as Joey could remember, had given her any real Wisdom. Joey took it with open arms and applied to a theatre school in Sydney. She planned to drive Sylvia up in early March when her acting course began.

It was dark now. The heat still remained, enveloping the valley in its oppressive embrace. A flurry of head torches were switched on around the campsite. Birds had found their resting posts on spindly branches, overlooking young children roasting marshmallows on open fires. A lone old woman across from Joey lit a cigarette. Her creased face glowed in the lighter's flame momentarily. Joey closed the boot of Sylvia and lay down, using her hoodie as a makeshift pillow. Before drifting off to sleep, Joey imagined the sound of an audience applauding, their claps raining down upon her in tiny droplets of cool water.

IV

By 6pm, Andrew was rip-roaringly drunk.

"You want me to open another bottle of wine for us, Deb?" Andrew asked, already wobbling his way from the living room to the kitchen fridge.

Regardless of Deborah's answer, another bottle would inevitably be opened. On the glass table in front of Deborah lay a large charcuterie board, picked at by vulture fingers. Loose grapes, broken crackers, sweaty cheese. Still in her bra and panties, she felt quite ridiculous now. It was enough to pique Andrew's interest when he first got home, and for a moment she could have sworn she saw something move in the crotch of Andrew's pants. But judging by his state of drunkenness, any hope of a night of passion was now well and truly extinguished. A bead of sweat trailed from the back of Deborah's neck and tumbled down the curvature of her spine. The heat was insufferable, even after dark. Thankfully, a slight breeze had emerged through the flyscreen door. The occasional breath of coolness offered up the briefest of opportunities for mental clarity in the fogginess of the heat.

Andrew stumbled back into the living room, barely holding onto the bottle of Sauvignon Blanc. His eyes had become glassy. He collapsed onto the couch next to Deborah and proceeded to slosh wine into his glass.

"Honey," said Deborah, "Don't you think you've had enough?"

"Well, Deb, come on now. Can't I have my fun?"

"Yes, you can," Deborah said coldly, "But this night was supposed to be about *us*."

"Yeah, I know," Andrew replied.

Andrew took a long sip from his glass and then set it back down on the table in front of him. Deborah looked at Andrew, ashamed and disgusted.

"Do you even care about me? Do you have to get this drunk to just spend a night with me?"

Andrew was unprepared.

"Listen, Deb, I know I've been distant. I know I have. I'm just still.... processing stuff," Andrew said slowly, careful with his choice of words.

"Yes," Deborah said softly, "But maybe it's just processing us now?"

"What'd ya mean?"

"Jesus Andrew! It's clearly chewing us both up inside!"

"No, it's not," said Andrew, insipidly.

"Look at me!" Deborah demanded.

Andrew looked away from his wife then took an even longer sip from his glass.

"What, now you can't even look at me? You don't speak to me; you don't touch me. I got all bloody dressed up for *you* and you care more about making love to that bottle of wine!"

All Andrew could do was shake his head.

"You're a drunk!" Deborah spat, "You only care about yourself."

"Fuck you," Andrew boiled over, "Fuck you. You think she was just *your* daughter?"

"It feels like it!" Deborah shot back, "Do you know how alone I feel? You left me, Andrew. All by myself. Not once did you even try to comfort me. You never came home. You lived at the pub. The fucking pub!"

"If I'm so awful, then why the hell are you still here? Why have you stayed?" Andrew barked.

Andrew downed the rest of his wine before topping himself back up. The truth was, it had never occurred to Deborah that she *could* leave. It was the house, she thought, that had kept her there. That room, the belongings, markers, reminders, strictures.

Annie was just 10 months old. An amorphous blob of soft flesh. In the bathtub, Deborah held a rubber duck in front of Annie, who was clearly more interested in the noise that was made when her small hands hit the water. Deborah set the yellow toy aside and cradled her daughter's small body in her arms. She knew just how to hold her. It was a mother's gift, a touch that she never knew she had until the Time had come.

The arms of her blouse were soaked through with the scent of tea tree oil that she had added to the bath. It rose with the heat, shimmering up from the water's surface. Deborah dipped Annie under, just for a moment, then brought her back up for breath. Annie's eyes shone brightly.

A knock at the door.

"Barry?" Deborah wondered out loud.

Barry was their next-door neighbour. On occasion, he would bring Deborah a basket of passionfruit. His vine would produce more than he needed. Andrew's favourite dessert was passionfruit pavlova – it was the perfect mix of sweet from the meringue and sour from the underripe passionfruit.

Deborah quickly took Annie's bath seat from under the sink and submerged it in the water. She lifted Annie into it and locked the front plastic piece in place.

"I'll be back soon," Deborah muttered, before rushing towards the front door.

Sensing her mother's absence, Annie cried. She cried for her mother, the warmth of her touch, the softness of her skin. She thrashed about and wiggled and screamed until she went red in the face. There was Barry's voice at the door, a dull drone, deflected by the impatience in Deborah's curt reply. Deborah sensed that perennial, primordial calling from her child in distress.

Annie bucked in her chair, lashing out and kicking, sending the plastic safety barrier into the water. In her haste, Deborah had failed to lock it in place properly. Annie immediately fell face-first into the shallow below. She opened her mouth to cry, but only swallowed water. Then, there was no crying. Eventually, her muscles relaxed, and her mind became subdued. Annie moved on to a place beyond this life.

When Deborah entered the bathroom moments later, she walked into a surreal nightmare. Pools of cold sweat itched in the crevices of her body. She heard her heartbeat in her ears. Face down, Annie looked to be asleep. And so, for a moment, Deborah just stood there, careful not to wake Annie. But then reality surfaced. Deborah screamed and lunged forward, ripping Annie from the warm water. Her small body hung flaccid over her mother's shoulder.

Deborah desperately smacked Annie's back in an attempt to clear the water from her lungs, waiting to hear her daughter cry again. It would have been the sweetest sound, to hear her daughter cry once more. But Deborah was only met by the slapping sound of skin meeting skin. By the time Andrew came home from work, Annie had been taken away. Deborah sat alone in the bathroom that night. Sleep never came.

"Deb?" Andrew asked, tapping his wife's leg impatiently.

Deborah's skin was marked with goosebumps. Her eyes had glazed over. It reminded him of the way she looked for the year after the accident – stupefied in a waking sleep. Existing; not living.

"Deb?" Andrew repeated.

Deborah walked into her bedroom, threw on some clothes, fished her car keys from the dresser and walked into the garage. Andrew drank the last of the wine when he heard Deborah's car speed down their dirt driveway. He could have called out to her, he could have chased her, he could have driven after her, but instead, he remained seated and held the empty bottle of Sauvingnon Blanc to his chest.

V

That night, both Joey and Deborah were woken from recurring nightmares by knocking. In her dream, Deborah sat tied to a wooden chair in front of an impossibly deep lake. She knew it was impossibly deep because the water was inky black in colour. The front of her chair was pulled forward by an invisible force, inch by inch. As she was lowered, she was met only with her own reflection, her skin tired from gravity's weight, her eyes opaque and afraid. When Deborah finally hit the surface of the lake, the cold that enveloped her was so violent, that a knocking sound rang in her head. It persisted as her extremities began to freeze and her heart began to slow. She saw only black and knew that she was all alone. At the bottom of the lake, she heard Annie crying over the sound of the knocking. Deborah bucked in her chair in an effort to loosen the ropes that restricted her. She screamed, but all that came out were water bubbles from her mouth. Then Annie's crying stopped.

When Deborah finally woke, coughing and spluttering, gasping for air, the knocking sound was still there. She rubbed her eyes and immediately realised that the knocking sound was coming from her motel door. Deborah, out of habit, reached over to Andrew's side of the bed. The red light of the radio read 2:47am. She stumbled out of bed, opened the door and was greeted by the motel manager who was so frazzled that he hadn't even buttoned up the front of his shirt.

"Sorry to wake you, but emergency services are evacuating the area," he said. "It isn't safe apparently. There's a bush fire coming through. I just got a notification from the SES. Everyone is gathering at Armstrong High School for the night. You know the way?"

Deborah just nodded and packed her bag for the second time that night.

Joey's recurring dream was more fractured than Deborah's. There were a series of moments, strung together in a seemingly illogical order. First was the flashing of blue and red lights that Joey saw out of her bedroom window. Then was the last goodbye before leaving for dinner that night. She saw her father pick her up and bring her into a bear hug. His stubble was itchy against Joey's forehead. She saw her mother bend down, kissing her on the forehead, and whispering, "We'll be back before you wake up, Joey." Knocking. Joey's babysitter, Rachael, rushing to the door. The feeling of knowing before being told. The fear in Rachael's voice. The sound of the kettle boiling. The photo of her parents on their wedding night that hung on the wall behind the stern police officer. His mouth moved but no words came out. The tears welling in Joey's eyes but not rolling down her cheeks. Then knocking again. This time on the boot of her car. Joey woke up startled, to find herself staring directly at the old lady whose face she saw glowing behind a cigarette earlier that evening. She stood back as Joey popped the boot.

"Is everything okay?" asked Joey.

"No, dear," the old lady said. "We all have to leave the campsite. There's a fire coming, the authorities say. We've all been told to sleep at Armstrong High School for the night. I thought I would wake you because nobody else was going to."

Joey thanked the old woman, who ambled back to her campervan amidst a sea of chaos – the mad unzipping of tents, the snapping of poles, the clinking of bottles tossed into eskies, children wailing, engines roaring. The sky was red and pregnant with smoke. Ash fell in droves. The one benefit of having no one was that there was no one to wait for. Joey left immediately.

By the time she arrived at Armstrong High, there were men in fluorescent vests pointing her towards the basketball gym. Ladies with solemn faces handed out pillows and sheets. Blue gym mats were littered across the floor to be used as mattresses. Families huddled together on the mats like packs of wolves, mothers attending to their young. Couples slept soundly together. Two brothers, five and seven, thought this was all just a very fun sleepover, and were wrestling on the mats. On the far side of the gym, under the basketball hoop, a woman sat cross legged. She was talking on the phone. *Maybe this is where the single people go*, Joey thought. Joey carried her pillow over and laid down near the woman on the phone. Joey listened to her conversation.

"I'm sorry, Andrew," the woman said, clearly irritated. "I only just saw your voice messages now. This all happened very fast."

A pause.

"What – What do you mean it's gone?... Gone completely?... And how about the dogs?... I'm at a high school for the night... No, it's okay... I said *no* Andrew... Okay, okay... Yes... Okay. I'll see you tomorrow... Bye."

The woman placed her phone on the mat next to her and exhaled loudly. Joey sat up and looked at the woman. The woman stared blankly at Joey.

"Is everything alright?" asked Joey. "I'm sorry, but I couldn't help but overhear your conversation."

The woman softened and slowly nodded her head. "Yes, actually," the woman said.

"Did your house burn down?" Joey asked, puzzled.

"Yes, it did," the woman replied.

Joey thought it was strange when she saw the woman smile. Deborah was visualising her house being enveloped by the fire – yellow, angry and ultimately beautiful in all of its destructiveness. She imagined the tin roof consumed by the heat, caving inward and falling down in a heap of smoke and soot. She imagined Annie's room containing remnants of her short existence, melting into a smouldering heap. And from these ashes, there would eventually be growth, life, another beginning. A sacred part of Deborah that she believed had long frosted over began to thaw out in the form of tears. They ran down her cheeks and dropped onto the blue mat.

"I'm sorry," said Joey, watching Deborah cry.

"No, it's okay." Deborah smiled and wiped her eyes. "It's really okay."

"Are you here alone?" Joey asked Deborah.

Deborah nodded and asked Joey, "Are you?"

Joey nodded.

"Then I guess we're not alone."

"No," said Joey, "I guess we're not."

Deborah and Joey eventually laid down on their mats as the fire raged on into the night, burning everything in its path, bringing with it a new, red dawn.

White Bird

24

From the basement window, I watch the snow fall from the Montreal night sky in thick, long sheets. Snowflakes shimmer and pirouette in front of the streetlights before making their landing on the frozen footpath below. Snow is still a relatively new reality for me. I grew up in Perth, where the only snow I'd see was the stuff that Uncle Fred snorted in the bathroom at family gatherings. When he told the family that he worked in "trading and dealing," they all assumed he operated within security markets. I was the only family member who knew what he was really up to. How else could he afford that Mercedes-Benz G-Wagen? Or his prized Gucci leather slippers?

I had seen snow in movies too. As a young boy, I'd reach out towards the television screen, hoping to feel it fall onto my hand. Snow might be a dreaded inconvenience for many Quebecois, but it's cold magic to me.

Li eyes the empty glass in my hand.

"Another drink?" she asks.

"Sure."

She takes the glass and fills half of it with rum and then tops it off with a dash of Coca-Cola.

"There you go. Coke with rum!" she grins, handing me the glass.

"More like rum with Coke!" I joke.

Li sniggers and sits down on Nik's knee. Nik is an American from New Jersey who is missing two front teeth after they were punched out in a fistfight. He hasn't bothered to get fake ones. You'd think he would, not only for aesthetic reasons, but also given his horrible lisp. He tells me that it's his fate, you see. That it's futile to change the path that has already been laid down for him. I'd argue that antagonising a macho Trump supporter at a Trump rally in Wildwood isn't "fate," but rather "stupidity." But who am I to tell Nik what fate is and isn't?

Li nestles her head into the nook of Nik's shoulder.

"You two really look like a couple," I say. "You know, you just kind of fit well together."

Nik runs his fingers through Li's long dark hair. I take a big swig from my glass and feel the hot rum run down my throat and glow right through me.

"I want to find that for myself one day. Someone who I just fit with, without even trying."

Nik leans forward and grabs my knee with a force that surprises me for his lanky build.

"Man, tonight's the night! I mean, fuck. You've been here a month and you've got nothin' to show for it. Think about it, man – there's plenty of hot French-Canadian chicks who *love* an Aussie accent. So, use it! Use it to find a girl with a good heart and a great pair of—"

"Nik!" Li scowls.

"What? I was going to say eyes!"

A nice French-Canadian girl with a good heart and a great pair of eyes sounded like a dream. I could imagine us drinking *chocolat chaud* by a fire on a cold, dark day.

My dating history has been patchy at best. I have been with a couple of serious girlfriends in the past, but ultimately, we dated out of a mutual fear of loneliness, not out of love. With each year that passes, I find that the romantic ideals that I harboured as a young teenager have slowly transmuted into a dark cynicism. At only twenty-four, I have come to believe that loving is purely a narcistic act, that a romantic relationship is simply a mode of validating whatever love you have for yourself.

I down the rest of my drink and Nik lights a joint, filling the small basement with smoke. Nik smokes so much that the stench of marijuana is inseparable from the space itself, embedded in the walls, the floors and the furniture. He rents the basement space on his dad's coin. Nik tells me his dad wasn't around much, so this is just guilt money. I watch the smoke drift upwards towards the smoke alarm, which has a shower cap tied around it.

"Improvise, adapt, overcome!" Nik declares, also looking up at the fire alarm.

His eyelids have already drooped over his red eyes.

"Okay," Li says, "*Allons-y!* We're not going to find your princess by sitting here all night."

So, I put on my jacket and head out the back door with Li and Nik in tow. Stepping out into the frigid night, I feel a great lightness enter my limbs as we turn down Laurent Street. I pull a cigarette from my jacket pocket, light it, and feel the nicotine buzz take over. I've found that it's best to smoke in moderation – you get the greatest value out of a nasty addiction. You just can't let it catch up to you.

I look over my shoulder to find Nik and Li, giggling, hand in hand. Normally that would be enough to make me sick, but tonight, I smile back at them. The snow pelts down against me, but I push forward, reaching out for my next shot at meaning in the dark. Nik tells me that a distant friend of his is throwing a party somewhere in the Chateau district. Without an address, we keep walking into a cold that stings our cheeks and brings tears to our eyes. Lining the street are opulent sandstone homes from a bygone era, complete with manicured gardens and picket fences, blanketed in a heavy coat of snow. *The suburban dream.* I don't buy it for a second.

I've seen heat maps of big homes just like these; most of the space is barely

set foot in. What's the point of busting your ass just to watch the dust settle

in empty rooms? When I am old and grey and my balls trail by my ankles,

I hope to own a small apartment that is actually *lived* in. Besides, it'll be

all I can afford as an English major.

Across the road, I hear the low thrum of techno music emanating from

a stately sandstone mansion. I call out to Nik and Li who are rolling around

in someone's front garden. Li has her hand down the front of Nik's jeans.

They sure are in love. All sheepish and smitten, they waddle over to me.

"That's it!" I point to the home across the road. "Don't you reckon?"

"Let's give it a go!" Nik says, enthused. "Worst thing that could happen

is that we walk in on a bunch of people performing a satanic ritual. It

happened to my oldest brother Johnny, that poor son of a bitch. He's never

been the same since."

We cross the road and follow the winding stone path to the front door.

I go to knock, but Li pushes the door open.

Music pumps from downstairs, sending shivers through the spines of

the furniture in the landing room. Laughter and drunken jeers echo through

the house, inviting us down the stairs, like some strange and demented...

satanic ritual. We stumble forward, zombified, entranced, as the arms of the music pull us towards the dark basement. Descending the stairs, we find that it's flooded with a deep blue light. The room is perfectly circular, with matte white walls sweating from the mass of moving bodies. Right in the middle of it all is a long-haired DJ pouring over his decks. The crowd responds in blurred movements. Nik and Li make for a leather couch pushed up against the curved wall.

A giraffe of a man, standing 6'5" in Doc Martens, floats into me like an empty chip packet caught in a gentle breeze. His brown eyes are framed by twin eyebrow piercings.

"What's up? Man?"

He laughs, a little wild laugh. I notice a small spoon swinging from his necklace.

"What's the spoon for? To measure sugar for your tea?" I ask.

"I don't drink tea! It's my ket spoon!"

"Ket?"

"Yeah, ket! Ketamine! They normally give it to horses, but it works great on people too," he grins.

"What does that even mean?"

"You'll only know, when you know," he winks.

He pulls a bag of white powder from his pocket and dips his spoon right into it. He hovers the small Everest of horse dust below my nose.

When I was in high school, I remember an anti-drug campaigner lecturing us about the dangers of drug use. She explained how she started smoking weed with friends and how that eventually developed into a full-blown heroin addiction. I remember swearing to my sixteen-year-old self that I would never touch a substance in my life. I would remain righteous and pure, prioritising intellectual pursuits over crusades of pleasure...

Ahhhh fuck it. I pull the spoon towards my right nostril and snort it all up in one go. The guy's eyes widen as he watches me.

"Oh shit!" he gasps.

My eyes also widen. "Oh shit" is generally not what you want to hear after snorting a mountain of an unfamiliar substance.

"What?"

"You know, it's not coke. I just... wow!" he laughs. "Man! I just didn't expect you to do the *whole* thing."

My heart rate immediately skyrockets. I grip my chest, believing that at any moment now, I will be struck by a sudden seizure. Seeing my body contorting on the ground in bizarre shapes, Giraffe Man would probably think I'd invented a new dance move.

"You offered me the whole pile!" I retort.

"Yeah, guess I'm pretty fucked!"

He takes a bump to demonstrate this.

"Well man, enjoy it. Buy the ride, take the ticket."

As the music builds in intensity and speed, I sense that I am on the verge of something quite profound. I figure now would not be the time to pull him up on his butchered Hunter S. Thompson quote.

"Sending good energy your way, my dude," he whispers, as if it were a Buddhist proverb.

He bends down and rams his eyebrow piercings into my forehead – *conductors of positive vibrations.* When the good vibe transfer is complete, he pulls away from me and glides into the crowd. I follow him in. Amongst the orgy of swaying bodies, the worry begins to melt away. I feel warm and home. Everyone, man and woman, smiles at me, all beautiful in their own twisted ways. I am transformed into a white bird, flapping my arms high above this toxic mess, free and untethered, flying into the night sky. I feel good. In fact, I feel fucking amazing.

As I am about to spread my wings to take off again, a girl grounds me by tugging on my arm. She stands just above five feet tall. Locked in her powerful gaze, I feel like a melted puddle of flesh. She starts dancing around me, rubbing against me, quick and petite, a dazzling haze of black hair and pale skin. I hold her in my arms and she leads my hands all over her body, enabling me to receive the power radiating from her hips, her navel, her shoulders, her breasts. The music soars higher and higher, and with her shifting against me, I feel a radiant cool spread all through my body. She turns to get a good look at me. I feel my face shifting into some sort of obscure object. Sweat drips from the end of my nose and splashes against the concrete swimming around my feet. Her face begins to move towards mine. *How to kiss?* Hunter would know. She leans into my left ear, climbs into the canal, and whispers, "Let us go then, you and I," in that beautiful French-Canadian accent.

An Eliot reference? A literary shuffle in my pants. Perhaps she just wants to leave this mad blue light? Either way, go, we shall. Although, here's the thing – my body has grown rigid and stiff, like an old piece of cardboard. So, she resorts to dragging me up the stairs, out the door and into the cold night. Under the moonlight, the girl's face is pink and flushed, and I spy a smattering of freckles across her nose. A slower song travels up through the basement, muffled by the front door. I let my arms fall over her shoulders, and she pulls me in towards her, looking up at me through feline eyes with great, dark lashes. Her flush has gone away now, replaced by a sheen of smooth alabaster skin. Her freckles pop. I watch them drift over her face in slow motion.

"Kiss me," she says. "I can't reach you."

I lean down and she rises on tiptoes to meet me. She tastes like liquorice. After a while, my tongue falls limp in her mouth. She takes it well and leads me away from the house.

"Do you want to come back to my place?" she asks.

In my state, I have no hope of finding my own way home.

"Yes," I say.

We make our way back to Laurent Street, down the quiet lonely road with neon lights that direct my attention to posters of scantily clad women and greasy poutine.

"Are we almost there? Do you have any beers?"

She says, "I don't have booze, but I have something better in mind."

I try to imagine what could be better than a beer right now. Maybe she has one of those Japanese toilets, with heated seats, air deodorizer and posterior wash nozzle. Now *that* would be better.

We finally arrive at her apartment building – a great, concrete monstrosity surging out of the snow. A homage to Brutalism, perhaps? We push through two glass doors and stumble into the foyer. The light is harsh, the air is stifling, and the ketamine is teasing me again. She calls the elevator. Before I know it, I'm inside an elevator hurtling towards the stars. The doors open with a ding. This must be space. She leaves. I stay, a broken robot in a human suit.

"Are you coming?" she asks, cocking her head to the side.

Reality finally arrives. She, a French-Canadian Princess, is letting me, a West Australian drongo, into *her* private castle, and here I am, floundering around like a live fish on a chef's chopping board.

"Yes," is all I can manage.

One heavy foot in front of the other and suddenly I'm safe inside her small apartment. It is everything that I imagined it to be: peachy wallpaper, dainty ornaments and plush carpets. Floor to ceiling windows offer expansive views of city lights, rushing cars and the odd person making their way home in the cold. She informs me that she needs to change in the bathroom. I ask her whether I need to change too, but I am answered only with the rough closing of the bathroom door. Exhausted, and perhaps a little defeated, I kick off my shoes and collapse onto her soft white bed.

An orange jar of "Brazilian Bum Bum Cream" sits on her bedside table. What the fucking fuck is "Brazilian Bum Bum Cream?" Is it for the hole? Is it for the cheeks? I open the jar to find what looks like dry-aged semen. I tentatively lower my nose and give it a whiff – smells like coconuts. I screw the lid back onto the strange concoction and stare up at the white ceiling, watching the interplay between light and dark, merging and separating in some arbitrary game of cat and mouse. Watching her ceiling, time and space become irrelevant constructs. How long has she been in that bathroom for? 5 minutes? 1 hour? 3 hours?

The bathroom door is flung open. She reveals herself to me. Dressed in black lingerie, with garters holding up sheer stockings, she strides towards me like a hungry tigress cornering its helpless prey. I sit up on the bed, but she pushes me back down and straddles me.

"No more games," she says, firmly. "I want you to rip off my lingerie."

Her threads do not look cheap. Premium Italian lingerie, I'd guess. I imagine the Italians to be good at these sorts of things.

"Are you sure?" I ask.

Her eyes are full of a thousand tiny flames. Of course, she's *sure*.

I go for the sheer stockings first, figuring those are the most permeable. I dig my fingers in and attempt to pull apart the black nylon. Unfortunately, the ketamine has completely fried my motor-skills. I give up and move towards her bralette, tearing at it in all directions like a mad savage. Again, unsuccessful. She looks down at me, incredulous. What did she expect? I can hardly unclip a bra sober.

"Forget it," she sighs, clearly upset. "How about you just tie me up?"

She pulls a black plaited rope from a drawer in her bedside table and lobs it my way.

"Here you are, cowboy. Let's see if those boy scout skills come in handy."

She spread eagles on the bed, her wrists up against the iron posts. It's one thing to rip apart some lingerie; it's a different kettle of fish to tie this crazed nymphet up in my hazy stupor. But who am I but a humble servant? I oblige, gathering the rope and looping it around her feeble hands, first the left, then the right, looping over and over until I am left with enough length on both sides to tie it off in the middle.

"Now! Fuck me! And do it well!" she commands.

I pull out my soft member and try mashing it into her opening. Nothing. Another mash. Nothing.

"Oh, come on!" she cries.

I jiggle him a little until he slowly responds.

"Just warming up," I murmur, fumbling towards her again.

This time it goes in, albeit, like some flaccid hotdog in a firm bun. Perhaps hotdog is too generous – a cocktail frankfurt, more like it. Her eyes light up. I finally feel weightless again, the white bird in me flapping up my windpipe and sailing out through my mouth.

"Now choke me!" she demands.

Now, I am not a violent man, but how could I not partake in such an act? I had failed her once. I would not fail her again.

"Harder!" she gasps.

My hands are white around her small throat. At this rate, I'm going to end up with a dead body on my hands. Imagine the headlines in the news tomorrow morning: *"DEMENTED LUNATIC DRUGGED UP ON*

HORSE TRANQUILISER MURDERS INNOCENT WOMAN IN A DEPRAVED SEXUAL ACT."

"Harder!" she pants. "Don't stop until I tell you to."

I choke harder, but as her face begins to turn a sickly purple tinge, I can look no more. Instead, I focus my attention back on the Bum Bum Cream, hoping somewhere on its bright orange labelling there will be a message for me. Halfway down the ingredient list, I feel her go limp under my strain. *Shit, shit, shit.* I start shaking her, as if to wake her from a deep slumber. I can't even call her by her name. She may have told me, but now, when I need it most, it completely evades me.

"Hey, hey, hey!" I shout.

Oh god, oh god. I can hear them printing the papers. The ink has well and truly begun to dry. Finally, she gasps and opens her eyes.

"Oh! Thank god, thank god!" I cry. "I thought I had killed you!"

"Did I tell you to stop? God, I was just about to finish!"

Despite my best efforts, I had failed her once more. She orders me to untie her from the bed before she storms off to the bathroom. I lie back on the sodden sheets, listening to the sound of water running, and dream of having more ketamine to numb the growing streams of inadequacy converging at the pit of my stomach. The tap is turned off, and I am torn away from my fantasy, left again to face my own romantic shortcomings.

But this time, I am determined not to face them alone. I slide off the bed and pace towards the bathroom in search of atonement. I knock twice on the door in quick succession.

"I'm really sorry," I say. "I failed you and I want to apologise."

Pathetic.

"Come in," is all that she replies.

She sits in an old copper bathtub with her back turned to me. The room is full of steam and the smell of wild berries. Upon my entrance, she faces me, eyeliner cascading down her cheeks from the moisture in the air. There is something fragile about her now.

"Please, join."

It isn't an invitation, more of a command. I can hear the tonal difference – a sign that the ketamine is beginning to wear off. Already naked, I slowly lower myself into the tub with her, careful not to make a splash and ruin the perfect stillness of the moment. She smiles kindly and nods her head, motioning for me to speak.

"I didn't want to hurt you, you see. That's why I stopped."

"You were right to stop. I just wanted to see how far you would go."

"Why?"

"Because I wanted to test your limits."

"My limits?"

"Yes."

"How did I do then?"

"You did okay. You tried. For tonight, you were enough."

Enough. She thinks I am enough. High up above the cold white snow, the 4am drunks, the loners, the vagabonds, the sodomites, in a bathtub with a French-Canadian girl who makes me feel like everything and nothing, all at the same time, I realise that *enough* is enough for me. I am with another human being, suspended in a unique moment of time, while the city trundles on below us, approaching the oncoming sunrise.

Little Dreamers

If the streets of Sydney could talk, Max wouldn't be able to hear what they were saying. It would just be a cacophony of noise, a constant susurrus, a melange of disparate voices, coalescing into one long conflated nonsense sound. It was the first day of December – Max's birthday. It was also Jake's birthday. The two brothers were born exactly three years apart.

Max searched for Jake's voice on Norton Alley amongst the low din of the city. He sat on the curb and held his hands against the hot pavement, waiting for his brother's words to seep through his skin, flow through his veins and ring in his ears. Along the alleyway, shards of broken glass reflected back at Max, winking in the sunlight. It was Max's lunch break. The cheap suit he wore sealed the sweat in. He felt the perspiration roll down his back, arms and legs in a desperate plea for escape.

When Max finally heard Jake's voice, he was struck by how soft it was. Barely a whisper. But it was his voice, just hollowed out. A voice without a body, without a character, without a face. Before Jake's words could be understood by Max, a Priest ambled down the alleyway with a cigarette in hand. He looked at Max, crouched over the curb, palms flat against the pavement.

"Are you okay?" the Priest asked as he approached.

Max looked up at the Priest, his face blinded by the sun. As the Priest sat down next to Max, his face came into view. It was a kind face, framed by horn-rimmed glasses. He looked to be in his middle-age. His thick hair was greying around the tips and he was dressed in a black cassock. Max watched as the Priest lit his cigarette and took a long inhale.

"Don't worry," the Priest smiled. "Cigarettes are my only vice."

Max laughed quietly. A woman dressed in orange workwear and a hard hat hurried past, glancing briefly at the two men sitting together. Max could smell the Priest's damp body odour cutting through his peppery cologne. In the heat of the day, the whole city stunk; the rubbish, the rats, the people, the smoke, all congealing and rising up in a great shimmering mirage.

"Gee, it sure is a hot one," the Priest said, reading Max's mind.

"Sure is," Max replied.

"If you don't mind me asking," the Priest began, before pausing to take a drag of his cigarette, "Why are you out here in this alleyway? In this heat? Shouldn't a man in a suit be spending his lunchtime in a nice, air-conditioned office?"

Max hesitated for a moment. The Priest smiled and nodded in an effort to reassure Max.

"It's okay," the Priest said calmly, "I am just a pair of ears, if you need them."

Max didn't speak for a while. The Priest started humming an orchestral tune that he had heard on the radio earlier that morning. Pigeons flapped their wings and pecked at a dirty sandwich that had been discarded in the alley. A bus pulled out of its stop on Elizabeth Street, its doors hissing shut. A baby wailed in a pram nearby. For most, the sounds and sites of the city were only cause for a dull headache, but to Max, the city was living poetry. He knew the city as his home. He knew the cracks in the road, the flickering orange traffic light on York Street, the bats that roosted in the Botanic Gardens, the fishy smells of Haymarket, the underpasses where you wouldn't be moved along.

The Priest's humming came to an end. Max turned to face the Priest, who he thought was handsome in a silver-fox sort of way. It was a shame that no woman could ever have him.

"Deep in thought, are we?" the Priest asked.

"I was just listening to the city," Max replied.

"Ah yes, marvellous isn't it? You know, it's such a shame that so few people take the time to really breathe in their surroundings. There is so much tremendous beauty around us, so many stories waiting to be told."

Max ruminated on what the Priest said. His life had become immeasurably busier since starting full-time work as a paralegal, but unlike most, he still took the time to admire the Spectacular Now. Connection to the present was how he slowed his mind.

"So," the Priest continued, "Would you like to tell me why you are sitting here? You have to understand, it *is* a peculiar site. Only drunks and vagrants hang about in this alley."

Max softened and leant back against the wall behind him.

"It's my brother's birthday today. That's why I'm here."

"Well happy birthday to him! Is he meeting you here?"

"He's already here," Max said.

The Priest furrowed his brow and stubbed out his cigarette on the pavement.

"Could you perhaps explain?" the Priest asked.

"From the beginning?"

"Please."

Max took a few deep breaths, then began.

"My brother's birth was one of my earliest childhood memories. He was born on my 3rd birthday. It was the best present I could've asked for. A brother. He was delivered in our bathtub at home. A water baby. I nagged my mother not to have him in water, for fear that he would drown.

But as soon as he broke the water's surface and I heard him cry, I knew that he was well and truly alive, dripping in water, gloop and blood. He was pale and wrinkly and glassy-eyed. I thought he looked like an alien from another dimension. My mother told me that he was perfect. She named him Jake.

"From that day on, my brother and I were inseparable. Whatever I did, he copied. Wherever I went, he followed. I was the only male figure in his life. You see, my dad went to prison shortly after Jake was born.

"Jake and I spent most of our youth on the trampoline in our small backyard. Tumbling, wrestling, jumping. We'd only stop when our mother called us in for thick slices of watermelon and fairy bread. We both attended the local primary school. It was a leafy school with painted water tanks, demountable classrooms and big gum trees that kids would climb at lunchtime."

"Well now," the Priest cleared his throat, "That does sound like quite the idyllic childhood."

"It was," Max continued, "But that all changed when my father arrived home after six years in prison. At first, it was exciting for us. I mean, after all those years of phone calls, we finally got to see him in the flesh. He was a big, jolly man who had an endless supply of energy initially. He'd lift us up onto his shoulders and spin us around, pretending that we were propellers on his helicopter body. He'd come to all our soccer games, yelling louder than all the rest of the parents combined. He was our biggest supporter. But over time, my childhood became less about bouncing on the trampoline with Jake and more about bringing my father longnecks of Tooheys New from the garage fridge.

"You know, it's funny how my father came back to alcohol. *Old habits die hard,* he used to say. You'd think he would have kicked the habit after serving all those years for a drunken manslaughter. He didn't talk about it much. All he said was that a man in a bar looked at mum funny, and that he deserved everything he got.

"Sure, Jake and I would hear stories about my dad from people in town, but we'd never actually believe he'd hurt anyone. That was until my mother came home late one night when I was thirteen. I watched it all happen through the crack of my bedroom door. Dad was asleep in his chair, a pie balancing on his belly. He was woken by my mother who was pottering around in the fridge.

"'Where the hell were you?' my dad asked.

"'Why the hell do you care?' my mum snapped back.

"My mother had never talked back to him before. There was something strange that came over her that night. At the time, I thought it was just the alcohol, but looking back all these years later, I think she just stopped giving a fuck, you know? She'd had enough. I couldn't blame her. Initially, he was good to the three of us. We used to eat fish and chips on the beach together and play cricket on the sand. But he never got a job, never really tried to either. He hardly moved from his chair – he just became part of it. A piece of human furniture, and just about as useful as one. Jake called it his poo chair, because it was brown and stinky. That's how I remember my dad. Glued to that poo chair, gut hanging flaccid over his Adidas tracksuit pants, ripped singlet, dirty fingernails, patchy beard, longneck in his hand, staring at the four walls around him. But on the night that my mum came home late, he peeled himself off that chair and lunged towards her.

"'I'm your husband!' He roared. 'I bloody well have a right to know where you've been!'

"He yelled so loud that it woke Jake, who gingerly shuffled up behind me to get a look through the crack in the door.

"'You know what?' my mother screamed, 'I don't think you want to know!'

"'Fucking try me, woman!'

"My dad got right up in her face. It was the closest I'd seen them together for a long time. He was so close to her that she could probably smell his revolting beer breath. To this day, I don't drink beer. Other alcohol, sure. But not beer. My dad reeked of beer. It stained his teeth a grimy yellow colour. When he would sweat, which was often, Jake and I could smell that warm yeasty stench pouring off his body while we played in the living room.

"'I've been at Jeff's place,' my mum said, unflinching.

"My father slapped my mother hard across the face. I felt Jake jump behind me. Jeff was the coach of my soccer team. He brought the oranges at half time. He chewed Big Red gum. His breath smelt like cinnamon, which I didn't mind. It was better than smelling like beer. Even after the Slap, my mother kept on talking, as if nothing had happened.

"'He's kind to me, he's gentle with me. He takes care of himself. He takes care of me!' she shouted.

"'Then fuck off back to him! I don't want ya here, and neither do the boys. Won't ya just fuck off?'

"So, my mother did fuck off, and she never came back."

The Priest cleared his throat and offered Max a cigarette. Max shook his head no. The Priest lit one and blew smoke through his nose. He leant back against the wall and inhaled deeply.

"Why do you think she never came back?" the Priest asked.

Max sighed.

"I think because we reminded her too much of the past. She started her own family with Jeff soon after, you see. And I guess we were just baggage of hers. Lost baggage that she didn't need anymore."

"Do you resent her for leaving?"

"No," Max said, "I would have done the same."

Max went on.

"After mum left, dad slowly eroded in his poo chair, spending his time watching replays of old cricket matches on telly. You'd think that the hole mum left behind would be partially filled by dad. Surely, you'd think, there was some semblance of paternal instinct deep within him. But there wasn't. There never was with my dad. We were just 'expensive' inconveniences to him. He handed me twenty dollars each week for food. I'd buy peanut butter and white bread for our school lunches each day. I'd cut the crusts off Jake's sandwiches because that's how Jake liked them. I'd make sure his clothes were clean and that he delivered his homework in on time. But of course, eventually Jake grew older, and I was no longer needed in that capacity. He grew fast too. By the age of fourteen, he was much taller than me. He had dad's height – perhaps the only good trait he offered. It was around this time that Jake and I came home from school one night to find the bathroom in a particular state of disarray. Our mirror had been smashed in, drawers had been flung open and the shower had been left on. Jake asked me what had happened, but I had no answer for him. I told him to go check on Dad while I made sense of the chaos. Our father was usually passed out in his chair when we came home from school, with the pie tin from lunch time still balancing on his gut. When Jake called me over in a panic, the first thing I noticed was the empty packet of Diazepam resting on his lap. Then a shout from the TV. Australia had just taken a wicket. While the Aussies celebrated, patting Glenn McGrath on the head, I frantically checked for my dad's pulse. Nothing. So, Jake and I sat in front of the TV for a while with dad, watching Australia topple the Sri Lankan batting order. You know, the funny thing is, eventually, we both started crying. He stunk of beer still. He never cared about us. He spent the only money we had on beer and frozen food. But we both still cried in front of that shitty television. We cried at his funeral too. We were the only ones there."

"But of course," the Priest interrupted, "It's only natural to feel great anguish when confronted with the prospect of our own mortality. If not for your father, then for yourself."

"Yes, you're right," Max replied, "I never thought about death much before then. I guess when you're a boy, you think you'll live forever."

The Priest pulled at his clerical collar. The synthetic material of his black cassock absorbed the worst of the sun. He inched further back against the cool wall.

"I'm sorry," Max said, noticing the Priest's discomfort. "Would you like to head inside? I can stop now."

"No!" the Priest protested. "Your story is unfinished. An unfinished story will make you sick. Please, you must finish."

The Priest was right. The more Max told his story, the better he felt. There was something distinctly cathartic, Max thought, about telling his tale to a religious confidant. Max continued.

"Shortly after my dad passed away, the house was repossessed by the bank, and Jake and I didn't have anywhere to go. If we had any other family members, they certainly didn't step forward. Who'd want to take us anyway? We didn't even have any friends who we could stay with. From a young age, my mum would call us the Little Dreamers. Jake and I lived in our own private worlds. We made up our own realities. It was safe. In our heads, we could be whoever we wanted to be. The possibilities were truly endless. That was where the Planet Games started. It was a game that Jake and I devised when we shared a room as boys. The purpose of the game was to create a planet, as if it were as real as Earth. We'd build out the planet together using our imaginations. One of the planets that we kept coming back to was Blupiter. Blupiter was inhabited by Bluetonians. All the Bluetonians were blue. Their blue skin was smooth and hairless, like a dolphin's. They rode on their blue dogs to work, who were fuelled by blue salami. The main job of each Bluetonian was to paint their planet blue. Everyone would pitch in as much as they could. The colour blue represented peace and unity to the people of Blupiter. At night, the Bluetonians would barbecue blue sausages and chops on the streets. The Bluetonians were free to live wherever they chose. Nobody owned anything in Blupiter. All was shared. And so on."

"You boys certainly had wild imaginations," the Priest remarked. "It's such a shame that as we grow older, we lose our propensity to dream."

"I suppose for most, that's true," Max replied, "But Jake and I never lost that part of ourselves. It was how we survived. After a while, a social worker came and moved us into public housing on the outskirts of Surry Hills. Without the distraction of school, our imaginations blossomed. We spent most of our time on the city streets, looking for inspiration for our planets. You know, it's funny… living on the streets brought us closer to the reality of a Bluetonian. There were no walls, no bedrooms, no bathrooms. Everyone who lived on the street became a sort of distant family member to Jake and I. They'd share their food, their shelter and their beliefs with us. We weren't the youngest there by any means, but we stayed the longest. In winter, you'd often see drifters making their way up the coast from Melbourne in search of warmer weather. During that time, our closest thing to a friend, or to a father for that matter, was a man named

Ted. He lived two doors down from us in the housing, but like us, chose to spend most of his time on the street. It was impossible to know how old Ted was, given his face was caked in a thick layer of street grime – dirt, car fumes, cigarette smoke. He had a croaky sort of voice and resembled a Santa Claus who'd spent too long in a prisoner-of-war camp. You know, white beard and white hair, but all ribs, elbows and sharp edges. We would find him chain-smoking cigarettes on the brick wall out front of our housing. I think what pushed us closer to Ted was the boredom. He was the only one who wanted to hang out with us constantly, and we had nothing to do. Aside from the nagging hunger, the restless nights and the insidious fear of oblivion, it was the boredom that presented the most danger. *Idle hands are the devil's workshop.* One day in early December, I found the devil, and God, in the form of a syringe."

"Heroin?" the Priest muttered.

"Yes," Max said. "But at the time, Jake and I didn't know exactly what it was. All that Jake and I were told by Ted was that it was good. It was just *good*. And you know what, Ted was right. I've since read books and talked to people on the street about their first time using. For some, they describe it as being touched directly by God – hypnotised by a catatonic rapture that permeates your mind, your body, your soul with a divine warmth. It washes away all the pain and misery, and all you can do is just lie there under that golden blanket of bliss. Others describe being invigorated like never before, dancing, singing, shot through with a languid looseness that takes you above those dank streets and heavy burdens of life. There is, of course, overlap in these accounts, and many others. But fundamentally, it was just *good*. The best kind of good you could ever feel.

"Ted put us in touch with a fat man named Mac, affectionately known as Big Mac, who invited us over to his dirty flat in Redfern. There, we met Jade, who was about half Mac's age. They were an unlikely pair, bound together by dependence: Mac dependent on Jade's body, Jade dependent on Mac's heroin. It was sad to see, but I guess they both got what they wanted out of the relationship. Jake and I sat on the edge of Mac's bed.

"'So, boys, who wants to go first?' Jade asked, holding the syringe in her hand as if she were a qualified doctor ready to administer a shot.

"Jake looked at me. I could tell he was nervous. His eyes were darting around the room, flitting around in his head.

"'It's okay,' I said to Jake, and then to Jade, 'I'll go first.'

"She tied me off with Mac's leather belt and worked her fingers around the crook of my arm. I saw my little blue vein rise up like a valiant fighter, ready for battle. She caressed my forearm tenderly, then plunged the cold needle into the vein. I felt a jolt seize hold of my body, ringing through me like an electric shock, before she hammered that dirty brown liquid into me. With each breath I took, the world around me began to lose its sharpness.

"Everything became soft and round and golden as I lay back onto the bed. I heard my mother singing to me, softly, as she once did when I was her boy. She whispered in my ear, told me that I was special. All my anxiety, all my confusion, all my heartache, simply evaporated into that golden air around me. I looked at my brother with all the love in my heart and nodded. I told him it was the best feeling he'd ever feel. Soon enough, he was lying by my side, cloaked in that golden air too, smiling, watching the dim ceiling light shower down upon us in a splendid waterfall. We both knew then that we had found our own planet. A golden planet, that was real and *ours*. A world only we could access, understand and experience together. But as the hours went by, the soft edges of our kingdom began to harden and grow brittle, before caving in on top of us.

"Despite the torturous come downs, that summer was the best of my life. Mac chased the sun up the coast, leaving Jade behind. So, it was just the three of us, living from hit to hit, not caring how we'd get it, just knowing that when we did, it would be glorious. Smack wasn't worth much. Besides, if it came to it, Jade would use her body as a form of exchange. You see, having that bright, slow rush once a day was the sunshine that Jake and I so desperately needed after all those years of darkness. It's sad that had to be in the form of a chemical, I guess. But it brought us closer than ever before. I'd feel his starving nerves become heavy and satiated with dope, see that big droopy smile wash over his face, as we'd slide back into our golden planet together. I thought I was doing right by him, you know. It was the happiest I'd ever seen Jake, and probably the happiest he'd even seen me. We would talk, properly talk, about all our fears. We'd remember mum together. We'd list all the things we missed most about her. Jake told me he missed dad. I told him that I missed him too. We laughed about the poo chair. Jake told me that he was grateful for me; that I was the best big brother he could have asked for. I told Jake I loved him; that it was him and I against the world. We would never have said any of this outside of our golden planet."

"Yes," the Priest interjected, "It seems to me that this drug-induced state of yours offered up the ability for you to be truthful with one another. A sanctuary for the freedom of expression. How long did this go on for?"

"Maybe a year or so," Max replied. "The last time I ever shot up was on a Tuesday. It was raining that day. The city was empty, with workers presumably sheltered in dry offices. Jade, Jake and I sat on Norton Alley. I watched a drop of rain slide down the slope of Jade's nose as she tried again and again to find the vein behind the yellow bruises on Jake's arm.

He pulled my belt tighter around his bicep and squeezed his fist so that his knuckles went white. Despite the December heat, his face was pallid and sickly. He needed it. The three of us had been on a binge and hadn't slept in days. All we had eaten was a small loaf of bread and an apple, shared between us, stolen from a vendor somewhere on Pitt Street. I pried the syringe from Jade's unsteady hands and plunged the needle into the middle of Jake's arm. His dopey eyes shot open, then softened upon the realisation that he was home, home, home. Away from the itching, the biting, the city cries, the screeching, the suffocating heat and the rabid stares. His dark hair fell over his wan brow, as he fell back onto the pavement and said, 'Thank you, Max. It's so nice here, so nice now, everything's gone gold again, won't you come…' before his words drifted out with him.

"The air hung thick and my skin crawled with bug bites. I wanted to join my brother in the golden light, but we were out of dope. Jade said she knew a guy in Dulwich Hill who had some. It was no use taking Jake with us. He'd only slow us down and Jade and I were both itching for a fix. That was how we justified leaving him alone in Norton Alley. Jake's eyes were closed now. His shirt was open, and his arms and legs were splayed out wide across the grey concrete. He had a small, smug smile on his face that contained the secrets of the universe. The rain did not fall on him, but around him, unable to penetrate the roof of his golden home. I told Jake that we would be back, but all he could do was squeeze my hand gently and nod his head."

The Priest pulled a handkerchief from his breast pocket and offered it to Max, whose cheeks were shiny with tears. The Priest too, was crying, but silently, for he did not want to interrupt Max's story.

"When Jade and I came back," Max sobbed, "Jake was still smiling, still splayed out over the concrete. A radiant urban angel. His eyes were closed. When Jade tried to wake him, she got no response. She kept yelling his name, trying to wake my brother, but I already knew that he was gone. Locked away now in that golden planet forever. Jade flipped out and ran away, fearing that the cops would somehow connect her to Jake's death. The rain poured down. I lay my head on Jake's chest, listening for a heartbeat that never came. I held his lifeless hand in mine and cried for everything that I was not, cried for the brother that I couldn't be, cried for the light that he would never see, cried for the life that he would never lead. There was only one thing that could bring me back to Jake. I felt around in my back pocket and pulled out the small baggie. Jade had taken the syringe, spoon and lighter with her, so I crushed the brown powder up even finer, dipped my key into the bag and snorted it. The gold began to wash over me as I lay back on Jake's chest and looked down the alley, angered by the busy people rushing by, all stuck in their own insignificant worlds. I yelled but no one heard me. No one wanted to hear me. Why would they? I was nothing to them but a sad story, a pathetic junkie, human furniture. I thrust the key back into the bag and took out as much as I could. It was too much, I knew that. It was supposed to be enough for both Jade and I. But I wanted to be with Jake so badly, you see, because there wasn't a life that I wanted without him. I took it all up in my right nostril and lay back again. Everything went so quiet until I heard a heartbeat. I peeled my head off Jake's chest and saw a young girl in a red dress tying her shoe at the end of the alley. A man in a black suit stopped by his daughter's side and looked back at me. His face was cloaked in shadow. But then a ray of golden light came down and shone upon him. My brother. Jake. All grown up now. It was his heart beating. He smiled. He smiled so brightly. And when he opened his mouth to speak, the whole world was covered in gold. Pure, fucking gold. Then it all went black again."

Max was crying so hard that all the Priest could do was put his arm around him.

"Let it all out," the Priest said.

Max did. It was the first time he had let it all out, for he had no one else to listen.

"That's why I've come back here today," Max wept, "Because I think that just maybe, maybe, I'll hear him speak, and he'll turn the world all golden again."

The Priest nodded sadly. In all his years of preaching, he had never found himself at a loss for words like this. And so, he placed the palms of his hands down on the concrete where Jake once lay, and sat there listening for one voice in a city of millions.

Revolution

In the smoky darkness, I sat by her side and watched her stare into the red mouth of the fire. She chewed a white marshmallow quietly and made herself small on the log. The bag of marshmallows lay open by her feet. I twisted a pink one onto the pointed end of my stick and held it by the flame's edge. In solidarity, a white marshmallow was thrust next to mine. She nudged against me and smiled. I looked into her eyes and was hopelessly caught, for those eyes sang of a light that I had never seen but had always known. We were just eighteen then, meeting for the first time in the backyard of a suburban house party. Seven years later, one grey afternoon in August, I sat across from Mia in a crowded café, and I couldn't help but feel that this time, they were my eyes too. Our years together had both blessed and cursed us with a shared vision of a history that followed us everywhere we went.

"We're like strangers now," she said.

I'd heard it once before. By the sea after our first break up. She had said it while she held seashells in the palms of her hands. Three months after that, we were together again. But this time was different. This time,

I sensed that she truly meant what she had said. Being "strangers" was no longer a benign platitude. And she was right, as she always was. Only one month apart and I barely recognised the woman sitting across from me. She had dyed her hair blonde and pierced her nose. But of course, as much as she tried to reinvent herself, she was, and would always be, the same Mia to me. The one who remained static in memory; a series of sacred moments that held steadfast against the changing winds of time.

She placed her cup of tea down on the table and tapped its side with her index finger. I knew very well that this was my cue to speak. We had cryptic ways of communicating like that.

"Of course, we are. But isn't being strangers a good thing now? A sign that we've grown?" I asked.

Her hands rested on top of each other. An angry red intent, the shape of a small crescent moon, had etched itself into the web of skin between her thumb and forefinger on her left hand. She hadn't been coping well without me. And it pleased me! It filled me with glee. She was struggling in uncertain tides, in desperate need of a buoy to keep her afloat. I could be that buoy. Without an answer from her, the silence began to widen the space between us.

We had never been lost for words like this. When we first met by the fire, we couldn't stop them from pouring out of our anxious mouths. A torrent of sentences that laid bare our aspirations, our insecurities, our dreams. I wanted to tell her everything. I wanted her to know who I was; all of me, untainted, unbiased, as pure as I was conceived, spoken with perfect exactitude. But language, by its nature, restricts, limits, confines. If she were to know me truly, we would have to fall in love. She would have to hold my pilgrim soul in both her hands and love it for all of its impurities. As the trivial and the sincere fell from her hurried lips, I had already begun to plan our future. I would be a celebrated journalist, and she would teach mathematics. We would balance each other perfectly like that. With every minute of conversation that glided by, this illusion of our future began to take on more intricate details, her words unfolding layers upon layers of iridescent imaginings. I was tangled in a future that hadn't even begun: obsessed, tied down, choking for air. And there was nowhere else I wanted to be. Oh, how I dreamed as a young boy that love would exonerate me from my suffering. That, with enough of it, all of life's tribulations would lift away from me and vanish into thin air. And so, I began to thread myself through Mia, and she began to weave herself through me.

"Grown?" she sighed, finally. "I haven't grown, Jack. I'm trapped in this fucking past with you. I can't grow here."

She plunged a spoon into her tea and stirred. I knew how she took it –

black with a dash of skim milk. I'd make her tea every Sunday afternoon, when we'd sit out on the deck under our frangipani tree. She'd always bake some sugary treat to accompany the tea – muffins, biscuits, cakes. But mostly she made scones. I'd often reminiscence to her about mornings at Grandma's as a younger boy. Waking up to the smell of butter, caramelised sugar, toasted flour. I'd bite into the warm fluffy dough and watch my Grandma smile fondly at me. Mia remembered this tale, and so, she baked scones for me most Sundays. She somehow managed to get hold of my Grandma's famous recipe, despite it being off limits to some of the more unsavoury members of my extended family. Every time I bit into one of Mia's scones, it was like being transported back to my Grandma's art deco kitchen all those years ago. When the afternoon turned to night, Mia would climb onto my lap and rest her head against my chest. She'd sing old Frank Sinatra songs and I'd nod off to sleep with her small warm body in my arms.

Her spoon knocked against the rim of her cup. She cleared her throat.

"So that's why I'm saying goodbye, Jack," she said.

"What?"

I felt a knot, the size of a fist, seize up inside my throat and tighten. I shifted in my chair and suppressed a groan.

"I can't be here anymore. It seems that I've got to leave to be able to move on," she continued, "So that's why I've decided to move to Paris. I've got a teaching position lined up there. Do you think it's childish of me? Just leaving like this?"

The waiter came to collect our cups of tea that were once warm but now unbearably cold. I wondered what narrative he imposed upon us. Two strangers in a coffee shop? Two friends? Two lovers? Two halves of the same whole? Perhaps he didn't think of us at all.

"No, I don't think it's childish. I get it. And I know you'll love Paris. It'll be a new start, I guess."

"Yes. That's right, a new start. And who knows who I'll meet there? Maybe a creative type?" she teased.

The knot pulled tighter inside me. Ambiguity had been a learned skill of hers, another stitch in her unending fabric. Was this a meagre attempt to make me jealous? Or was it a calling for me to fight for her to stay? I could always see myself straddling these peaks of her possible truths, lost in the cloud of uncertainty, constantly walking the tightrope, to and fro, to and fro.

"Yeah, maybe you will," I deflected, hoping she wouldn't hear the anguish in my voice.

Maybe he is here, now. Maybe you already know that. To and fro, to and fro.

"Why now?" I asked, then pleaded, "Why do you have to leave now? Can't you just stay a little longer?"

She opened her mouth to speak but then the rain came. It pelted down on the corrugated iron roof overhead. That was the beauty of the rain. It demanded to be heard. The silence fell again between us. The knot twisted and bulged inside me. A baby boy in a highchair at the table across from us began to wail and, in spite of his mother's best efforts, threw his stuffed zebra across the floor, hitting Mia's ankle. She looked down at the well-loved toy and smiled before handing it back to the apologetic mother. It was a smile that I knew all too well: one suffused with melancholy, tinging the edges of her lips with a cold, blue stain. I'd always wanted a family, you see. I was an only child. Mia's parents had broken up when she was young. Her dad was an opioid addict. She didn't talk about it much, but there was clearly a tenderness there. Sometimes I could feel it when I held her – loose, jangling pieces of a past buried deep in the cavern of her chest. Her dad didn't even call for her birthday. She didn't care for a family. As much as I tried to bring her around to it, she just wouldn't budge. Sometimes at night I'd dream that a child was growing inside Mia's womb. Udder-heavy, she'd stumble forward, swatting away soft toys and stacks of nappies in search of oily French fries wrapped in yesterday's newspaper. Our black cat Jerry would stare at me through green eyes, as if to say, *am I, Jerry, the black cat, replaceable?* When her water would finally break, I'd imagine her fingernails digging into my wrist on the drive to the hospital. How wide her mother bearing hips looked in that sterile bed. Container of creation. And what a marvellous creation he would be. All 3.5kg of him. Ripe and juicy, flesh like a hairless peach. I would take him from Mia's breast, his breath hot and milk-sour, hold him against my chest, receive him. He would be the best of us, and we would be the best of him.

"Can we just go outside?" she asked over the rain's patter.

"But it's raining," I said.

"Exactly."

I paid for our pot of tea and followed her out into the rain. Her perfume hung heavy in the muggy air. She was wearing *the one I liked*, the one that smelt earthy and wild. The cloud lifted a little from the peak of ambiguity.

In a matter of moments, the rain had caused her golden hair to become drenched and bedraggled. She stepped away from me and began laughing, sticking her tongue out to catch the rain.

"Won't you join me?" she asked.

I couldn't. With her tongue pointed skyward, I could feel the weight of parallel universes looming above me. I had seen Mia do this before. Whether in a dream or a past life, it didn't matter. And what was I to do if

I could not bear witness to more of these intimate moments? My imaginings tortured me again, occasionally offering fleeting glimpses into a future unlived. But as Mia walked towards the station, these narratives collapsed upon themselves and showered down upon me with the rain.

All I could do now was follow her. I was used to it. She was a brisk walker that had a feverish intent behind every step. She acted as if she knew where she was going even when she didn't. I loved to follow her on our way to work. I remember the way her hips would swing from side to side in pencil skirts. Her calves were smooth, perfect ovals. I'd catch up to her and hold her hand. She'd pull off down the path to university and kiss me goodbye as I ventured to my office alone. We had walked this route together so often that it became a routine. A choreographed dance unknown to the world that existed outside of us. As far I was concerned, a world outside of us was not a world at all. And then, one day, she decided that she no longer wanted to walk to work with me. She said she preferred the bus. Wanted to sleep in. Hated the sound of traffic. Couldn't stand the car fumes. Like any rational, caring partner, I respected her decision and decided to walk alone. On the day that I intended to propose to Mia, I saw her with another man in a café during my morning commute. She was laughing. Beaming! He rested his hand on hers. He was also beaming. I stood across the road and watched these two strangers in love. The engagement ring burnt a hole in my jacket pocket.

On the way to the station, the rain began to fall more heavily, and our words finally came back to us. Mia told me that her father reached out to her after all these years. She told me that she was slowly repairing the damage that had been done to her. We talked about the night we ate popcorn while we dangled our feet over the edge of a bridge. And the time we went wine tasting in the country and I spilt Shiraz all over her white dress. And the time we fostered a black cat called Jerry and Mia knitted him a scarf. But we never talked about the fights. The tears. The lying. I suppose we like to see the stars in the night sky before we recognise the darkness around them. After I saw Mia with the other man, she would feel lifeless in my arms. Like some part of her that was mine, and mine alone, was gone, missing, given. I didn't even confront her about it. I was so deceived by my devotion. I merely thought of it as a minor blemish on our otherwise perfect relationship.

Nearing the station, we idled under the roof of a dingy grocery store. Though the wind howled and bit at the side of my face, and though my bones grew cold, I didn't dare move for fear that the last seams of our thread would completely unravel.

"Why do you even want me to stay?" she asked

"Because I love you," I said.

"Why?" she asked.

"Because I need you in my life," I said.

"But you don't *want* me in your life?" she asked.

"No," I said. "I just need you."

She bit her lip.

"I don't want to go, but I can't stay either," she said.

We began our last leg to the station. *I'd be so much better at it this time, I wanted to tell her. I would! I would! If only I could go back and reset it all. And Mia would change her ways! She would! She would!* But time only lurched forward, and the rain just carried on filling the open holes inside both of us, until we finally made our way through the gates of the station. On the platform, we stood among commuters hurrying past us.

"This isn't it, is it?" I asked.

I looked down at her and she looked up at me and we both smiled at each other, knowing, all this time knowing, that everything in our world was already utterly and beautifully lost.

"Goodbye," she said.

"Goodbye," I replied.

But neither one of us left.

Night Swing

Harry Gant is most content between the hours of 8pm and 10pm at night. On his apartment's balcony, overlooking the quiet neighbourhood park, Harry sits on a small plastic chair and labours over his miniature wooden boats. After a ten-hour day managing financial assets behind a shield of wide-screen monitors, the intricate process of shaping, sanding and polishing his little boats in the summer night offers joyous respite from the endless monotony of Excel spreadsheets. It is the rigour of the process that Harry finds so alluring – the precise tenets required to transform balsa wood blocks into perfect miniature replicas of grand sea-faring vessels. Keelboats, skerry cruisers, catamarans – Harry has tried his hand at them all. In a society that values outcomes and output, productivity and profitability, Harry's wooden boat sculpting serves no commercial purpose whatsoever. His boats exist only for their own aesthetic value, beautiful and radiant in the flickering fairy lights woven around his balcony railing. A nettle tea and two cream biscuits sit on a wooden table at arm's reach. Removing his glasses and wiping the sweat from the bridge of his nose, Harry pops a biscuit into his mouth and looks out into the night. A lonely swing is ruffled by the gentle breeze. Even from his balcony, Harry hears its vexing squeak. A homeless man sits on the park bench opposite the big metal slide, with a bottle of wine dangling precariously from his hand.

Two balconies below Harry's, Greg Chambers sits on a large wicker chair, nursing a beer. He watches the same homeless man on the park bench with a child-like curiosity.

"Gracie, come have a look at this bloke!" Greg hollers.

"One moment, just making myself a nice cocktail!" Gracie calls from the kitchen.

The homeless man gazes at his playground surroundings. He scratches his scraggy beard and takes a long pull from the wine bottle. Gracie emerges through the balcony door with a vodka lemonade in hand – her idea of a *cocktail*. She sits in a wicker chair next to Greg and takes a sip from her drink.

"What is it, darl?" she asks, shifting her hand onto Greg's knee.

The homeless man lifts his t-shirt to inspect his belly button. His finger extracts a piece of fluff.

"It's like he's a bloody actor or somethin', the way he is carrying on. And all we've gotta do is just sit back with our drinks and watch," Greg beams. "For fuckin' free! Drinks and a show!"

Gracie edges her way towards the balcony railing. A dingy light hangs overhead, attracting an eclipse of moths to its dull glow. The homeless man gulps down the last of the wine and sets the bottle on the bench. He eyes the swing shifting on its hinges.

"You watch, Greg. I bet he starts avin' a swing!" Gracie says with a big grin, before necking the rest of her *cocktail*.

The homeless man ambles over to the swing and lunges for the plastic seat, but his feet trip him up onto the spongy rubber matting below. Before he hits the ground, Greg's booming laughter can be heard across the neighbourhood. It is so loud and menacing that birds asleep in park trees scatter from their perches. Gracie and Greg hear a shuffle from somewhere above them, followed by an audible grunt and the sliding shut of a balcony door.

Gracie nods upwards, "Neighbour doesn't want a bar of it."

"Fuck em," Greg snaps, before gulping down the rest of his beer.

He reaches under his chair and drags the four remaining bottles in their cardboard box across the concrete pavers. He takes one by the neck and opens it in the palm of his hand.

Gracie sits back down next to Greg and rests her head on his shoulder. She is assaulted by the smell of Greg's body odour but is already too drunk to care. Besides, it's Greg's smell. Her Greg. The pair watch the homeless man steady himself and get back on the swing, rocking back and forth with a lugubrious expression on his face.

Two storeys up, Harry sets his alarm for 5am, hangs his Wednesday suit over his desk chair and switches off his bedside lamp. He falls asleep to the slow squeak of the swing, oscillating on its tired hinges.

***

Early on Sunday morning, Harry wakes to find that there is no almond milk in the fridge. Harry blinks in disbelief. There is always almond milk in the fridge on Sundays. In fact, Harry measures his daily milk intake every day and records it on an Excel spreadsheet in order to avoid milk supply issues like today's. It is in Harry's best interest to measure and record. After all, it is how Harry maintains his excellent order. An organised life and an organised mind exist in a symbiotic relationship. So, with an average of 122ml consumed each day this week, it is therefore an impossibility to be without milk on this Sunday morning. In a panic, Harry rummages through the fridge, shifting fermented vegetables and knocking over bottles of home-brewed kombucha. Nothing. He checks the crisper drawer in case the milk has miraculously slipped in with the fresh produce. Still nothing. He closes the fridge door then opens it again, hoping that the

1 litre bottle will somehow shuffle forward and declare itself.

But of course! In the fog of his morning brain, Harry neglected to consider the milkshake he made for himself last night. Harry finds a tall glass in the sink and examines the chocolate syrup sediment still stuck to its inner edges. A double-choc peanut butter almond milkshake. He crouches below the sink to find the empty milk bottle in the recycling bin. Harry consumed the rich shake in bed, naked, while scrolling through photos of his ex-wife – a guilty pleasure that he tries to keep out of mind the next morning. Regardless, milkshakes on Saturday evenings are an occasional indulgence that serves to offset the intensity of his weeks: an innocuous sugar fix that keeps Harry's mind in a state of perfect equanimity.

Harry pads across his sunlit living room and enters his bedroom, catching his long body in a large mirror fixed to the wall. In only red boxers, he tenses his traps, his quads, his biceps, his toes. It is a body that he believes to be attractive in its non-invasiveness. It doesn't scream for attention, yet it is firm and tidy. He shoots finger guns at his reflection then tucks his smoking index fingers into the elastic waistband of his boxers. Gliding across to his closet, he slides open the wooden doors to reveal chromatically ordered shirts, set against pants matched on pre-determined criteria including texture, material and colour. He picks out a mauve polo shirt and slips into his complementary tweed pants. Harry swivels around to find his own reflection again. In the morning light, the skin on his face is pallid and taut, stretched tight against his high cheekbones. He moves closer to his reflection and examines a spot above his right eyebrow. A pimple? A blemish? Perhaps a pre-cancerous spot? A mental note is made to arrange a doctor's appointment, which is filed neatly in the back drawer of Harry's hippocampus. Taking hair gel from his bedside table, he lathers the gloopy slime through his dark hair until each strand it thoroughly coated. Then begins the slick back process with his whale bone comb. He begins combing the left side, then the right, then the top. Always in that order. The hair around his temples has begun to recede. This harrowing first sign of male-pattern baldness plagued Harry initially, prompting a phone call to a doctor in Turkey who offered to carry out a hair transplant for what Harry deemed to be a reasonable price. But being single in his early thirties, the ripe age for finding a life-long partner, the lengthy recovery time spent outside of the dating scene could not be risked. After a quick spritz of Chanel cologne and a once over in the mirror, Harry bounds out the door in search of almond milk, with a Sunday spring in his step.

***

The cold bottle of milk perspires in Harry's hand as he waits in line at the local corner store. A fan in a rusted metal cage wheezes gusts of air that disperses the smell of stale sweat and overripe produce around the store. In front of Harry, Greg rocks back and forth on his heels. He holds a six pack of beers in his hand. The bottles clink together. Over the beeping of the cashier's scanner and the whirring of the conveyer belt, Greg lets out a long yawn. He didn't sleep last night. When product needs to be moved, sleep can wait. Greg worries that by the time he gets home, the beers will have lost that cold, refreshing taste that he so desperately desires. A couple of beers on the balcony will inevitably send Greg spiralling into a deep, dreamless sleep.

Next in line, Greg plonks the beers in front of the cashier. She offers a smile. Greg is too tired to return it.

"That'll be twenty dollars, thank you sir," she says sweetly, which appears particularly incongruous with her sordid surrounds.

Greg tosses her a crumpled twenty dollar note and grabs the beers.

"Thanks darl," he says, before stopping to pick up a catalogue at the exit.

Harry sets down the bottle of almond milk in front of the cashier and fishes his wallet from his pocket. He gives her his best smile, which she returns with an even wider one. A dating seminar that Harry recently attended advised that eye contact is the single most important factor in communicating confidence to women. He widens his eyes and stares directly into hers.

"Ah, that'll be four dollars, thanks," she says, slightly perturbed by Harry's laser stare.

Her lips are painted a glossy peach colour and her hair is tied in a bun that looks messy in a neat sort of way. Harry hands her a five dollar note. He grabs the milk.

"Keep the change," he says, giving her the "head nod and wink" manoeuvre that he also learnt about in the seminar.

"Ah... actually," she begins, "We can't keep the change..."

But Harry doesn't hear her. He's long gone, head held high, milk tucked under his arm, soaking up the auspicious rays of the morning sun. Birds chirp overhead, cars rush by, mums walk briskly with ergonomic prams, gossiping about what liberal candidate they fancy for the upcoming state elections. Fifty metres up ahead, Greg has already cracked open a cold beer. He guzzles it down as if it were a player's Powerade at half-time of the NRL grand-final. Harry watches the big man up ahead turn left down Waratah Road. Strange, Harry thinks. He wouldn't forget seeing a man like Greg. He's what Harry's mother would describe as "rough around the edges" – shoddy mohawk, sun-bleached tattoos snaking up bulging arms, dirty white singlet. In a small, upper-middle class suburb of inner-west Sydney, Greg stuck out like a sore thumb. Where were his RM boots? His pressed linen shirts? His oat milk flat whites? Drinking alcohol on a Sunday morning – ludicrous!

Greg stops at a bin to toss his empty beer bottle. Harry maintains his walking speed. They make brief eye contact. Harry offers a smile, Greg does not. Greg continues flat-footed along the path until he peels off at Number 18 and walks up the flight of stairs to the intercom. He fumbles around in his pocket for a key. Harry tiptoes up the stairs behind him.

"What the hell," Greg mutters, feeling around in his back pocket.

"You need me to let you in?" asks Harry.

"Yeah, that would be great, champ."

Even for Harry, "champ" was a little insulting, a term mainly reserved for young boys in sports uniforms. Greg eyes Harry's lean frame, his dark hair greasy under the beating sun. A real corporate wanker, Greg thinks. He follows Harry into the musky foyer and up the blue-carpet stairs.

"So how long have you been living here?" asks Harry. "Haven't seen you around before."

Greg hesitates behind him.

"Ah, just a couple weeks mate."

"And what brings you to the area?"

"Change of scenery."

They reach the landing on the third level.

"This is me," says Greg.

Harry stops and turns around to face Greg, who is bent over and panting.

"Pesky stairs, aren't they?" says Harry.

Greg just nods and pants, eyeing the condensation dripping off the milk in Harry's hand.

"Ah shit!" winces Greg.

"Everything okay?"

"The milk. I forgot the fucking milk for my missus!"

Greg stands upright, towering over Harry in the cramped landing. Sensing an imminent intrusion on his personal space, Harry edges back.

"Say… you reckon I could borrow some milk, neighbour?"

Greg gives a wide smile for the first time. The warmth of his smile is so discordant with his tough-guy appearance that Harry almost drops the bottle of milk then and there.

"Son?" Greg cocks his head to the right.

"Su-sure."

Harry stands there, bottle slipping from his sweaty hands, a burning sensation growing in his cheeks. Greg steps forward and Harry flinches.

"Jeez, didn't mean to scare ya matey. I was just going for the door."

Harry straightens, readjusts, clears his throat.

"Oh yeah, totally," he says, casual as anything, "It's almond milk by the way."

"Of course it is," Greg grimaces.

Greg knocks twice. An initial patter of feet on carpet, and then the door swings open.

"Aha!" Gracie exclaims, locking eyes with Harry, "A friend! Oh goodie, come in."

Before Harry can refuse, he is led by Gracie down the hallway and into the living room. Her bleached blonde hair, frayed at the ends, is so long that it just about covers the Southern Cross tattooed above the waistband of her low-rise jeans. Her hoop earrings dangle with each step she takes.

"I'm Gracie!" She beams. "What brings you here?"

Greg cracks another beer and discards the bottle top on the ground. Harry watches it roll past discarded lingerie, two inflatable sex dolls, empty bottles of spirits, lighters, coins, hand sanitiser, plastic baggies, a bowl of cereal. Harry looks at the two of them, studying him like prey.

"Milk. I'm just here to g-give you some milk. I don't mean to pry," Harry stutters, and rubs the back of his head, "My name is Harry. I live two flights up from you."

"I forgot it, ya see!" Greg chimes in, "And then Muscles here happens to walk in the door behind me with a bottle and I ask him if he could spare some."

"Well, aren't you sweet!" Gracie says, playfully.

Harry offers the milk to Gracie who examines the label on the bottle.

"Now, how the hell do they milk almonds?" she sniggers, shaking her head all the way to the kitchen.

Greg shuffles awkwardly on the spot.

"Ahh, you want to come out for a beer on the balcony?"

Harry doesn't know what to say. He doesn't even drink beer. But by the time he is seated on the balcony in Gracie's wicker chair, it is too late. A cold beer is forced into his hand. The pair clink bottles. Harry takes his first sip but struggles to keep it down. To Harry, beer tastes like yeasty sock juice.

"So, what about you? How long have you been living here?" Greg asks.

"Two years and twenty-eight days," replies Harry.

Greg burps and laughs. He squints at Harry, who looks out to the park.

"You live alone?"

"Yes. I do now. I used to live with my wife."

"Where is she now?" asks Greg.

"She left me," Harry says without a hint of emotion.

"Fuck her then!" Greg declares.

Harry nods emphatically at Greg. With newfound confidence, he brings the beer to his moisturised lips and takes a long sip. But the burning on the way down causes Harry to cough it back up and set his beer down between his legs. On impact, beer foam shoots straight up over the lip of the bottle, erupting onto his pressed tweed pants. In a futile attempt to quell the liquid onslaught, Harry bends down and covers the opening of the bottle with his mouth, filling up his cheeks with froth. Greg laughs so hard his chair tips back and he hits his head against the balcony door.

"Jeez, no wonder she left you! Ya big clutz!" Greg gasps for air between laughter. "Gracie, bring this boy out a rag for his mess!"

"Don't get too excited out there!" Gracie calls back.

Harry hangs his head in his hands. Greg places his hand on Harry's shoulder and smiles his goofy smile. Not a corporate wanker, just a corporate loser. There's a difference, and Greg appreciates this difference.

"It's okay mate, shit happens. You just gotta laugh at yourself sometimes," Greg offers. "Can't control shit like that."

Harry looks at Greg's big sincere face. And for the first time in months, Harry smiles. Not just the forced mechanism of stretching lips over face — a routine that Harry has religiously practiced in the mirror at home. No.

Harry smiles a smile that disseminates warmth all through his veins, radiating outward in a million fractals of euphoria.

Gracie hurries outside with the rag in hand. She goes straight for Harry's pants, dabbing at the dark stain on his crotch. As she leans over him, Harry notices a large tattoo on the inside of Gracie's forearm for the first time; a heart with a sword through it, encircled by a frilled ribbon that reads, "Live to Ride." As Gracie dabs away, Greg chuckles and winks at Harry. Not sure how to respond, Harry takes up Greg's advice and laughs. Necking the rest of the beer and placing it by his feet, Greg also laughs until Gracie eventually joins in. Their laughter echoes across to the park where a group of young boys play soccer with a tattered ball. White cockatoos reel in wide circles overhead, dipping their heads to catch wind of the laughter on a late Sunday morning.

***

In the lingering glow of a Saturday afternoon, Harry sits on his balcony amongst his beloved wooden boats, an ice-cold chocolate almond milkshake in one hand, a cream biscuit in the other. The sun dips below the industrial factories that cast yawning white rings of smoke across the pink sky. On his phone, Harry stares at a photo of his ex-wife, his face smooshed against hers. The photo was taken on a romantic holiday in Bali that ultimately ended with them sleeping in different rooms. He thought he understood her, that their relationship could be controlled, categorised, compartmentalised. That she was a cell in a spreadsheet, able to be manipulated at will. But she changed, she made Harry feel small, and he accepted his fate, unwilling to push back in fear that he would push her away. And when he finally did decide to push, she was already halfway out the door. That was love, or at least Harry's experience of it.

As the pastel sky is engulfed by the descending curtain of night, Harry finishes his milkshake and thinks about the cashier at the corner store. Her messy bun. Her busy hands. Her smile. That smile. It could melt snow on the coldest winter day.

On the street, raucous teens tear up the footpath on skateboards, sinking tins of beer and smoking cigarettes. The scents of onions frying, potatoes baking and meat grilling are carried from neighbouring apartments up to Harry's hungry nostrils. He wonders what Gracie and Greg would be cooking. In the weeks since their first encounter, Harry often pops in for a beer with Greg at night. Even though he still despises the taste, he does it to strengthen the bonds of their friendship. He does it just to see that little twinkle in Greg's eyes.

A nascent siren wails in the distance. Probably a drunk driver. As the darkness creeps in, the siren grows loud and angry, drawing the skaters to a halt. Across the road, an old woman stands on her balcony with an oily wooden spoon in hand. Harry hears a knock at his door. Then another knock, followed by a gruff yell. Greg. Unmistakably Greg. Heart pounding, Harry races to the front door, his speed fuelled only by an encroaching paranoia. He swings the door open and meets the frantic eyes of Greg.

"You need to help us get out of here! Right now!" Greg splutters.

"What? What do you mean? Why? Why?"

"Why are you asking so many questions?" Greg sneers.

Harry takes a step backward.

"Are those police for you?" he asks.

"Listen, Harry," Greg says stiffly, "I move stuff around."

"What stuff?" Harry asks.

"Cocaine, mostly. Sometimes speed, sometimes molly when I get my hands on it. I never mess with the fucked shit – no heroin or meth. I'm ethical like that, ya know?"

Gracie pleads in a voice so sweet it almost knocks Harry off his feet, "Please, Harry. We've got to go now."

Her arms are open by her side, like those of a lost, helpless toddler. The "Live to Ride" tattoo on her forearm shines in the overbearing light of the landing. The puzzle pieces begin to form a whole in Harry's clouded mind. The tattoo. The baggies in the house. Greg's "rough around the edges" look.

"You're... you're... *bikies?*"

The word hangs in the air briefly, before it's swallowed whole by Greg.

"No shit."

The siren looms closer. These are the only friends Harry has now.

"Okay, okay, okay," Harry says.

Harry scurries to his bedroom, retrieves his car keys and races to the door. He takes a deep breath.

"Let's go," Harry says, cool as hell.

Harry's blue Toyota Prius is parked behind the apartment block. Even though Harry has been driving it for five years, he remains impressed with its fuel efficiency and safety features. Clambering into the backseat with Gracie behind him, Greg clearly does not feel the same way.

"God, I'd almost rather be caught by the pigs than drive around in this pussy on wheels," Greg mutters.

Harry pretends not to hear him as he pulls out of the driveway and down the street. He observes the speed limit. The sirens are close now.

"Jesus, please go slower. Not like we're in a fuckin' rush!" yaps Gracie.

"I won't be speeding," Harry says. "I haven't got a speeding ticket in my fifteen years of driving, and I don't intend to get one now."

Gracie and Greg fall silent in the back. As Harry turns the corner, two police cars speed around the bend, sirens blazing, almost t-boning Harry's Prius.

"Duck," Harry yells to Gracie and Greg.

They do as he says. He checks his rear-view mirror as the police cars pull into their apartment driveway. The fear has left his body. He is in control. He is at the wheel. He is the master.

Instead of asking where they'd like to go, Harry says to Gracie and Greg, "I'll drop you at the bus terminal."

They just nod. Harry turns on the radio. Smooth FM. Michael Bublé's soft Canadian voice enwraps him. Gracie and Greg choose not to make a comment. On the main road, Harry finds a police car in his rear vision mirror. Its lights turn on, pretty red and blue.

"Drive, drive, drive!" Greg screams, also seeing the flashing lights in the rear-view.

But Harry continues to observe the speed limit, even as the police car speeds up behind him.

"What the hell are you doing?" Gracie yells.

The police car signals for Harry to pull over. He obeys. Greg and Gracie swear at Harry. Greg even kicks the back of his seat. But Harry remains unshaken. After all, he *is* following the road rules. The pair of bandits try and make a run for it, but both are intercepted by police before they can get away. Now the two vehicles that Harry saw earlier have pulled up behind him. As Greg and Gracie are slammed against the bonnet of his Prius, Harry begins to laugh. Slowly at first. A tickle in the back of his throat. But then it morphs into something larger, something loud and morbid, bubbling upward from his belly. He laughs for the end of his shitty marriage, laughs for his meaningless career, laughs for the only friends he cannot keep. No longer a man, no longer Harry Gant, he is just a small wooden boat – an aesthetic object, to be moulded and shaped by the hands of fate. Long after Harry himself is cuffed and pushed into the back of the police car, long after his Prius is towed, long after the homeless man takes his post on the squeaky swing in the empty park, Harry sits in his holding cell and laughs, harder than he ever has before.

Wide Open

All the light in the world shone from his salty eyes as he held my small hand in his.

"We're going to go in together," he said, his voice muffled by the waves in front of us.

I turned to my mother on the shore, nursing my baby brother Billy. She smiled and waved. I turned back to my father. Bronzed and strong. The sea spat and hissed. I clung to his leg.

He gave me a gentle nudge before taking a necklace from his pocket. He looped it around my neck and rested his hand on my shoulder.

"See, now you have one like dad."

I looked down at the shark tooth dangling from the black leather cord. It glinted in the sunlight.

"Our necklaces are connected, just like us. It means that no matter where you are, dad will always be with you."

I stood straight and let go of his leg.

"That-a boy!"

He swung me onto his back and we galloped towards the oncoming waves. I dug my legs into his sides and squeezed my arms around his thick neck.

"Wooo-" I screamed.

And then all noise ceased to exist. I had been in this environment before, six years earlier, freediving in my mother's womb. Together, my father and I dived into a liquid world of weightless suspension. In our cocoon, I could make out little fish darting around our ankles. Then they scattered as a wave broke overhead. The force knocked me from my father's back onto the sandbank below. I did not struggle. I submitted myself to the ocean. I had come from water. This was my home.

Before long, my father's hand came plunging down towards me. He took me from my home and swung me over his shoulder, all wet, slippery limbs. Lying me down on the shoreline, I coughed sea water and smiled. My father laughed.

"You're a funny little bastard," he said to me.

He laughed a little more, picked me up, and held me against his chest where the wind couldn't get to me. Bronzed and strong. He contained me.

***

Nothing stirred in my empty fibro home. When you're under water, there's movement. The sound of sand shifting in its seabed, waves plummeting against the shoreline, currents moving around you. My home collected dust. I watched it fall through the first light of day, drifting lazily towards the wooden floor and settling there. I finished my beer, grabbed my car keys and pushed off into the morning, following that great, yawning coastline in my Pajero.

Open, lonely roads at dawn. The smell of the sea flooded through my window. I lit a cigarette and savoured that first nicotine rush of the day. Driving for kilometres without another car in sight, I felt as if I were the last man on earth, taking the final road to nowhere, oblivion caving in all around.

Then, Ashurst Nursing Home appeared out of the arms of the trees. It was a hell of an eyesore; a grimy, purple painted compound, caked in salt and rust, corroding from the outside, slowing falling apart, just like its occupants did inside.

I laughed.

How could I not laugh? How could you not find humour in your own impending mortality? If you couldn't, where would that leave you? A miserable bloke, I'm sure.

I wondered if my father was laughing, as he rotted away in his room.

The lady at the front desk told me I could find him on the East Wing. The last room on the right, overlooking the cemetery across the road. It was a short journey from life to death, she joked. My father was facing away from me when I entered his room. Sitting on the edge of his single bed, he stared out at the cemetery. All bone now, from a distance, he could have passed as a young boy, if not for his unkempt white hair. But up close, he told a different story. All colour and vitality had drained from his body, leaving behind a decaying relic of the man he once was.

"Dad?"

The wind battered against his window. A single breath escaped him.

"Dad?" I repeated.

He still refused to look at me.

I removed the shark tooth necklace I had been wearing for thirty-eight years. I placed it on his bedside table. He turned finally, looking at the necklace before looking at me.

"Wait…"

I left his room and shut the door behind me.

***

My earliest memory of my father? His hands.

Strong, long fingers protruding from rough palms. They resembled those hairy tarantulas you'd see on Animal Planet. When I was nine, I saw their fuzzy, black legs wrapped around our neighbour's throat. He had poisoned our lemon tree.

My father's hands weren't just for violence. They were healing hands too, he told me one morning on his way to work.

"What's a gino-kwa-logest?" I asked from my booster seat.

"A gynaecologist. Gy-nae-colo-gist. Well, Charlie, a gynaecologist is someone who helps women." My father chuckled before adding, "Every man would dream of having my job."

"Why would every man dream of having your job?" I asked.

"Well, ah," he chuckled again, "Let's just say, you get to use your hands to heal women."

I looked at my own feeble hands, soft and clammy. All I knew was that I wanted hands like my dad's – strong hands that could heal women.

At the hospital, my father left me with a nurse named Amber, who escorted me to the nurse's quarters. I sat next to her and watched her type on the computer. *Clickity-clack, clickity clack.* Her acrylic nails were painted a glossy red. Certainly not healing hands with those vicious nails.

"Those nails look very sharp," I told Amber.

She smiled at me.

"Do you not like sharp nails, Charlie?"

"Well, it just means that you can't heal people, that's all," I replied.

Amused, she stopped typing all together and swivelled around in her chair to face me. "What do you mean?"

"Well," I began, "My dad has hands that can heal women. But his nails aren't sharp like yours, or red! Those nails look like they could scratch."

"Healing hands," she giggled, "Is that right, Charlie?"

"Yes. Has he healed you?"

Amber shifted in her chair.

"Your dad heals lots of women," she said.

She swivelled back around and resumed typing. If my dad truly did heal lots of women, maybe he was healing one at that very moment!

"I have to go the bathroom," I told Amber.

I slipped away and made my way down a brightly lit corridor until I found a door that read "Dr. Phillip Gates: Gynaecology." I opened it slightly, so as not to disturb my father at work. Through the small gap in the doorway, I could just make out a woman with blonde hair sitting in a funny chair. My father was shifting between her legs with his hands on her body.

This must be healing.

***

There he went. Shot right past me. Carved across that big blue face of the wave and whipped his tail at the crest. The older blokes whistled and jeered at Whipper as he paddled back to the point, a wide grin plastered across his freckled face. We called the older blokes "sea dogs" – always smelly, always in packs, always yapping.

"You're up next," Whipper said to me.

I eyed the eight-foot sets rolling in from the back. They looked like mountains to a thirteen-year-old. Sharp rocks to my left, jutting out of the coast, waiting to claim me as their next bloody victim. I could make out a bunch of girls on shore, watching me, taunting me.

"I don't know. I might just go in," I replied.

Whipper splashed water at me.

"Come on, Charlie! Stop being such a wimp. You see those girls watching?"

I looked at the girls, drawing figures with their toes in the sand.

"You reckon they'd want you if you paddle in with your tail between ya legs?"

On the beach, I saw a stream of red hair. The water began to surge beneath me, and I paddled. I paddled. Hard and fast, plunging my arms deep into the cold, blue water below. The wave carried me, and I pushed up on my board, gliding across the arching face of the wave – flying, weightless.

There was the red hair, flapping in the sea breeze like some flag of victory. The wave built overhead, swollen with volume, and there again, I saw her hair, now a red flag warning me of danger. My father taught me to respect the ocean but at that point in time, I couldn't give a rat's ass about it. I just longed to be tangled up in that hair. I imagined it'd smell like vanilla, or maybe strawberries.

Swallowed. Sucked deep inside the ocean's churning belly, encased in a liquid womb of rage. I waited. And then, I was tossed onto the shore, out of the womb, into the world.

A smiling face leant over mine. I coughed up sea water. She knelt down beside me, her hand resting on my rising chest, her long red hair falling over my face and body.

"I'm Liz," she said.

Life entered parts of me that I never knew existed.

***

Chicken and veg. Again. Overcooked chicken. Soggy carrots and peas. Dad was late to the table. Just Billy, Mum and I. Billy stabbed at his chicken and took a bite.

"Billy! Wait for your father!" Mum scowled.

"What's the point? He's been more than ten minutes in the shower. You know what it means when he takes long showers," Billy retorted.

"The longer the shower, the worse the day." Mum sighed, "Fine. Start."

Billy tucked in. I nibbled at a pea. I knew exactly why my father took long showers. I imagined him smiling as the sexual fluids of the blonde-haired woman sluiced down the shower drain, while Mum ironed his shirt for the next day.

"Good peas," I offered.

"Thanks, hun."

My father towel-dried his hair as he came thumping down the hallway, tossing his sodden towel over the back of the couch before seating himself at the head of the table. He eyed his plate and exhaled slowly.

"This looks great…"

Mum slipped some peas into her mouth. Dad scanned around the table.

"Charlie. Billy tells me you've been seeing a girl?"

"Yeah."

"And are we ever going to meet this young lady?"

When I met Liz, I promised myself that I would never introduce her to my father. I would never give him the opportunity to *heal* her.

"I'm not sure," I shrugged.

"Well," he leaned back in his chair, "*I'm not sure* whether it's a good idea to have a girlfriend in your final year of high school. You should be focusing on your exams, not on some teenage fling."

"Just because something else gets in the way of my relationship, doesn't mean that I'd walk away from it."

"What do you mean by that Charlie?" Mum asked.

"Well—"

Down went my father's plate. I saw it coming before it happened. I had a struck a nerve, as I had intended. As I learnt in biology class, when a nerve is particularly sensitive, the muscle can spasm and cause involuntary movement. In this case, my father swept his plate off the dinner table.

He bent down, picking mushy peas and carrots from the carpet, not bothering to search for his chicken. He sat back at the table and began picking at his food with his hands. The same hands that had, hours before, caressed another woman in a cheap motel room. I couldn't stomach another mouthful.

***

The line was hardly moving when I got there. A baby wailed in his trolley seat while his mother unpacked groceries onto the conveyer belt. An old man with a bottle of green cordial grumbled from behind her. Two young boys with a bag of gummy bears bantered behind the old man. The cashier scanned through the items, not looking up once at the exasperated young mother who now stood before her.

I waded through the canned food aisle until I stopped at the best available vantage point. She was focused as she took the items and swiped their barcodes, placing them into a brown paper bag in one fluid movement. If you never looked hard enough, you'd never recognise her true grace. The shoppers sure didn't. Her navy branded shirt was iron-pressed, her long blonde hair was pinned up in a ponytail, and her eyes shone a piercing blue. I studied her, like a detective of sorts, looking for certain attributes, certain proofs, that would confirm what I already knew but couldn't accept as truth.

Her eyes flicked towards me from behind the cash register. The line had dissipated. I buried myself among cans of tuna.

"Are you alright? Need a hand with anything?" she asked, as she approached.

She was tall for a woman. Her name badge read "Tracey."

"Nah, sorry, I'm alright."

"You been around here a lot recently, haven't you?"

"Yeah."

"That hoody you're wearing is really baggy."

"Yeah."

"Awful lot of room to hide items under?"

"What?"

"You've been coming in and out for months, not purchasing anything, just watching me, seeing if I see you. Seems a bit suspicious, don't ya think?"

"No. No, I just— look, I haven't done anything. I just like supermarkets, that's all."

"And you expect me to believe that?"

"Yeah."

She eyed me all over with that blue gaze of hers, then stopped on my shark tooth necklace.

"Ha," she murmured.

"What?"

"The necklace. Who gave it to you?"

"My dad."

Her eyes narrowed in on my face, then they softened and widened. She didn't say anything more. She knew I knew.

I looked her dead in the eye as I shoved tins of tuna into my pockets and walked out the sliding doors of the supermarket. She didn't follow. She didn't move, not even when the queue began to build again.

***

Voice message received today at 3:41am:

Charlie. Listen. It's your old man here. I know it's been a while. I'm sorry. I know you don't want to talk to me, and I respect that. I'm only calling because, listen, it's been eating me up inside. And with my memory deteriorating more by the day... I wanted to tell you before I lose it completely...

***

Liz rested her feet on the dash. Red hair blowing in the winter breeze. We were twenty-four. Vagabonds. All we needed was an open road and all the adventure that came with it.

Somewhere south of Byron, Liz pottered around in the small kitchenette of our campervan. I watched her cook spaghetti in her underwear, snapping photos of her movements. She pulled a piece of spaghetti from the pot and shaped it into a pasta moustache, laughing, always laughing. *Click, click, click.*

You could only capture her through a lens for so long.

Up close, on the bed, colliding, with cold noses, goose-bumped flesh, warm lips. Told her she's my home. Told her she'll always be.

***

It's about Liz, Charlie. I'm doing you a real service here. I know you might not see it like that, but I hope someday you will. I'm sorry I'm calling so late. It's just, I needed a couple drinks was all. I'd tell you in person, but, hell, I wouldn't drive all that way down the coast for this. Listen... marriage is hard, Charlie. And sometimes you slip up. I know you always knew about Tracey. But what you didn't know is that I had a child with her, just after you were born. Fuck... look, Charlie...

***

Liz waved at us from the shore.

Her belly was loose and pale. She wore a red Santa hat and a yellow bikini. I gently waved Casper's small arm back at her before lowering his feet into the shallow blue water. His eyes widened; a primordial recognition of sorts – *home*. He giggled and kicked his feet as I held him up by his arms. A wind picked up from the point and swept towards us. Casper wailed. I held him against my chest. I contained him.

Liz walked towards us.

"Does my little boy like the sea?" she cooed.

"He sure does. Just like his dad," I said, wading out of the ocean.

I gave Liz a salty kiss on the cheek. She pulled her Santa hat off and placed it on Casper's wet head.

"Merry Christmas, my darling boy," she whispered into his ear.

We sat down on the sand. Casper reached for Liz's breast and latched on.

"I never expected a Christmas by the beach," she remarked.

"Why is that?"

"Well, I always imagined we'd have a big family lunch, like I did when I was a young girl. My mum would always bake ginger cookies for dessert. But those special lunches didn't last long. No more cookies after she left.

God, I can't stand the smell of them now."

Liz looked down at Casper and stroked his forehead with her thumb.

"Promise me we'll always stay together," she said, "For Casper's sake. I don't want him to grow up in a broken home like us."

"I promise. You two are all I care about in this world."

Liz kissed me, then lifted Casper from her breast and kissed him on his nose. The sun began to set, and everything began to glow, warming the three of us right through to our centres.

***

…. Liz is mine and Tracey's. I'm sorry Charlie. I really am. You know, when your mum showed me the wedding photos, I couldn't believe it. I was gobsmacked. You'd kept her hidden from me for so long, how could I have known? But I thought I'd let it carry on, you know? No one would get hurt that way. You two seemed really happy, and with Casper on the way… I just didn't know how to tell you. But listen, one thing I've learnt in life, is that you've got to live with your eyes wide open. There's no other way, Charlie. The truth will always catch up to you eventually. I know what I'm doing is right. It's the truth. I'm doing right by you. Please call me when you get this message. I love you, son.

The voice message beeped. The harshness of the morning light crept under our curtains. Liz slept soft against me. Casper was silent in his cot.

Then the walls began to strain. Growing water pressure, pushing hard, in all the walls around me. A broken water valve perhaps? Cracks appeared; gyprock splintered. Sea water began to seep out from under the floorboards, edging towards Casper's cot. I stumbled forward and leant over him. His sheets were drenched. I tried to scream, I tried to cry, but all that came from my mouth was salty water, spilling onto my son's dewy face. The walls finally burst. I was flung hard against the bed, as my son and wife were lifted away in the ocean's torrent. Falling, swallowed. Scattered photographs floated by me as I was pulled down deeper

Liz with her spaghetti moustache

A new-born Casper in my arms

A day at the beach with my dad

As the room turned dark and still, I sat at the bottom of my bedroom, eyes wide open, waiting. Waiting. Waiting for his hand to pull me to the surface and into the light.

ABOUT THE AUTHOR

Connor Lindstrom is a writer from Sydney, Australia. His life-long passion for words has led him to study literature at The University of Sydney and McGill University. Now a recent graduate, *Wake* is his first collection of short stories. Previous stories of his have been published in *ARNA* and *The University of Sydney Student Anthology 2018*.

9 780645 167306